Fables from the RAFFLES HOTEL ARCADE

Fables from the Raffles Hotel Arcade

A COLLECTION OF SHORT STORIES

Angsana Books
SINGAPORE

Published by

Angsana Books
SINGAPORE

for
Raffles Hotel (1886) Pte Ltd
1 Beach Road
Singapore 0718

Cover by Mangosteen Designs and T G Toons
for Raffles Hotel (1886) Pte Ltd

Angsana Books is an imprint of
FLAME OF THE FOREST Pte Ltd
Yishun Industrial Park A
Blk 1003, #02-432
Singapore 2776
Tel: 7532071

Printed in Singapore

ISBN 981-3056-72-X

Publisher's Note

FOR a long time East and West have met at Raffles Hotel and made this cultural confluence a source of inspiration for story-tellers.

The stories in this volume reflect this and will take the reader through varied settings and a range of voices and styles. However, the Hotel holds within its walls countless stories that have remained untold. Now that this book is published, we hope more of these tales will find their way to print. This should help to explain more fully the phenomenon that is Raffles Hotel for fiction has always been an excellent medium to convey atmosphere, sentiment and occasion.

THE PUBLISHER
SEPTEMBER 1995

Contents

The Man in White

K O LANDELL-JONES

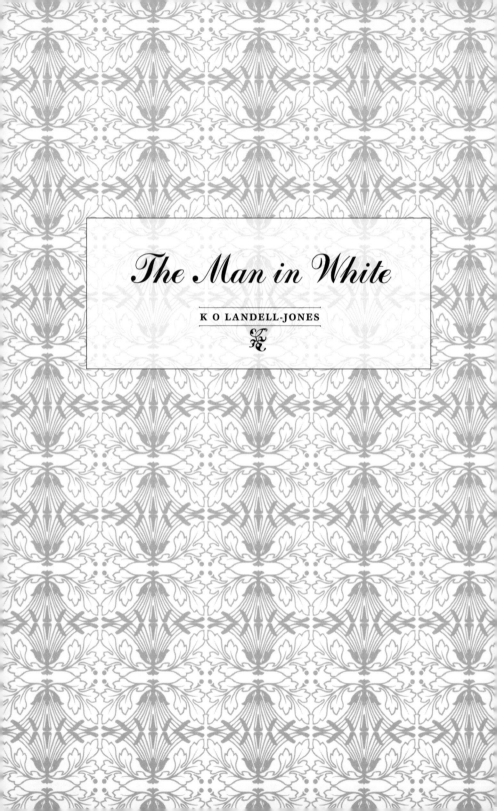

I HAD the great pleasure of introducing my grandson to Raffles Hotel in November 1993. I can't say I was following a long-standing family tradition, however; nor will I pretend I wouldn't like to see it become one. I had the joy of first seeing Raffles with my grandfather; so when John — this, my first grandchild — was born I told myself that, when he was old enough, I would introduce him to the legend that has enriched my life. I had the hope that, despite the nonchalance of today's young people, it might commit him to its spell — as it had committed me.

I had told him a great deal about Raffles and Singapore over the years. However I knew, no matter how much he had heard, that the story would be incomplete until he had added his own impressions to those that I had passed on to him.

He would learn, as I had, that Raffles changes and grows a little more fascinating every day as each new guest makes a contribution to the tapestry of human emotion and experience that is the foundation of this grand hotel.

When we arrived, he for the first time, I for the fifteenth, I found I shared his anticipation and excitement, having discovered long ago that no two visits were ever the same.

As we stepped from the car I stood looking at the remarkable work of restoration that had been completed since my last visit. Raffles had regained the splendour and freshness that I remembered so vividly from my first trip in 1930. But it looked much bigger: perhaps in keeping with the reputation that had gone on growing over the years; or, it may be, merely to remain visible amongst the mass of less appealing structures surrounding it.

As we neared the entrance I looked at the assortment of people waiting for different things: a taxi, their car, a friend — or just for the spirit and the mystery of Singapore to invade them.

On the top step, outside the front door, was a gentleman wearing a white suit. It attracted the sun and, although he was surrounded by people with less modestly coloured clothing, made him stand out strongly from them. He was surveying the hustle and bustle passing the oasis of tranquillity from which he watched. He would, I dare say, have seen as considerable a number of chilling winters, and welcome summers, as I had.

When our approach interrupted his survey and his eyes met mine I studied them carefully. Understandably, alas, they did not contain what I was looking for. His resemblance to one of my most treasured memories was remarkable in every other sense. The eyes, however, were merely those of an ordinary man, one who only saw what was in front of him, without question and with insufficient admiration.

He was, unfortunately, one who believed that wealth created its own wisdom and modernity brought new icons to excite the senses. Perhaps it was a presumptuous appraisal on my part; but when you read my story you will learn, as I did, the wisdom of believing in your own truth and the importance of being bold enough to look beyond the obvious to find it.

I shall never forget that seventh day of January 1930, when I first arrived to stay at Raffles. I saw a man whose features are still engraved upon my mind.

He had stood, like this modern stranger, on the top step, wearing a white suit. But his eyes had locked onto my grandfather and me as soon as we emerged from the car, following us as we walked towards the door that he appeared to be almost guarding. As we passed, his scrutiny gave way to a modestly gracious smile and a barely audible "Good afternoon". My grandfather, requiring a louder voice to attract his attention, must have appeared very rude as he marched intently inside. I smiled in return, partly to acknowledge the greeting, but primarily to release the excitement our arrival had created in me.

His eyes had not just been watching us. They had been analysing and appraising. Not in a critical way: quite the contrary. It seemed as though he had a desire to know us, that he had been expecting us. I had the feeling, absurd as it must sound to anyone who had not been so scrutinized, that in the few seconds it took us to cross the short distance to him he had learned a great deal about us. I felt, from his smile, that he had enjoyed the process and was not disappointed by the subjects.

His face had remained quite emotionless until fleetingly altered by the transient smile. The expression in his eyes was not one of rude curiosity. It was of interest and concern — as though we were very precious to him and it was his duty to know and understand us.

When we reached the reception counter and my grandfather took care of the paperwork, that I as a twelve year old could not assist with, I turned back and watched the man in white. He was still looking out across the entrance. He had not moved. I believe he had learned what he wanted to know about us and was probably learning just as much about whoever or whatever now attracted his attention.

I didn't see him again for a few days. My grandfather kept me busy with daily tours to the different parts and attractions of Singapore, which I found totally fascinating. I had not travelled abroad before and, of course, Asia was so different from everything that I knew in London.

There is still a wonderful difference, even today, that modern buildings and western clothes cannot camouflage. However, in the thirties, apart from some colonial architecture and numerous inappropriately attired white people, the scene was much less orderly and the mores of European culture remained a subject of wonder and amusement, not something to be emulated or allowed to interfere with a local's constant quest to earn a living.

On the third day we visited some acquaintances of my grandfather. They lived in Bukit Timah, far from Raffles, but I would not have been surprised to see a tiger leap out and set upon one of the people we periodically saw walking beside the roadway, such was the mastery of nature in the parts of the island that man's meddling had not yet spoiled. With my keen desire to witness something few people had seen, the journey passed all too quickly; and of course I did not see anyone attacked. It was a great disappointment. However, I realised there was a saving grace about seeing nothing on the way out, and that was the opportunity awaiting on the return journey. So, with this positive thought in mind, I arrived looking very civil, wearing a broad smile on my face, no doubt immediately dispelling our host's fears of having an uncontrollable child let loose in the house for the afternoon.

Incidentally, that evening, having had an uneventful trip back, I confessed to my grandfather what I had hoped to see. Naturally he admonished me, and it was then that he told me the famous story of the tiger under the billiard table. Needless to say I spent the rest of the stay at Raffles worrying for my own safety whenever grandfather left me alone or I had to make the long trek to my room, which I assure you was bolted securely every night.

I'm afraid I have forgotten the name of the people we visited. The man worked for a trading company, dealing mainly in copra and rubber; hence the relatively distant location of their home, which was on the company plantation.

He was a good many years younger than my grandfather and he had the great fortune to share his isolation with his wife, a very pretty and charming woman from London. She must have been marvellously understanding, and very much in love, to allow herself to have been plucked in her prime from what then seemed to be the centre of civilisation, and transported across the world to this beautiful but lonely spot.

She had lovely honey blond hair and large green eyes. Soft eyes. I quickly discovered that the couple had no children and I remember thinking what a shame it was they had none. Her compassion would have been very comforting after grazing a knee or falling from a tree. The pain would not have survived her sympathetic expression, her inherent kindness absorbing all misery completely and immediately.

Two of the three pairs of eyes I remember so clearly — as if just looking away from them to write these recollections — were those belonging to the lovely woman and to the man in the white suit. One pair offering the kindness of humanity; the other so ably demonstrating the acuteness that man's intelligence could attain.

Another thing I shall never forget about the outing was an unexpected encounter with the daughter of the people who worked in the house. A Chinese girl. I think a little older than I was, she was shorter than me but her chest already pushed away her blouse in a manner I did not associate with girls of my own age.

I had gone for a walk in the garden, realising almost immediately that the horrifying spectacle that I had so wanted to see on the journey out might very well, at any second, become a first hand account as I had, unwittingly, placed my fate in the hands of the Ultimate Judge the moment I wandered from the safe confines of the house. I constantly told myself not to be afraid of tigers and wondered, involuntarily, what other terrible boy-eating demons might lurk in the dense jungle. My only consolation was the great admiration I knew my bravery must have inspired in the minds of the adults I had left behind.

When I heard something rustle the undergrowth I immediately thought of my mother and father and all my school chums whom I would never see again. It was the first time I had associated myself with death. That emotion has stayed with me as well, becoming all too familiar in recent years. At the time it was a terrible sensation, though mercifully fleeting.

As I looked in the direction the noise had come from, with a fierce expression designed to frighten away the awful beast I was certain would pounce at any second, I saw quite the opposite of what I had expected. The girl's face appeared from behind a tree.

It was a pretty, shyly smiling face. I was transfixed

The girl's face appeared from behind a tree.

by the niceness of it. The smooth tanned skin resting against the rough grainy bark took on an angelic appearance, a deserved quality enhanced by my gratitude at seeing it.

She stepped slowly into the open, revealing the blossoming blouse and a slim body tapering to tiny feet. Apart from "Hello" she spoke no English. While I found her strangely appealing, it was her face that fascinated me. Thick black hair, surrounding flawless olive skin, shared its glow and perfection; and the sun found its sheen to its liking, constantly bouncing off it into my eyes. The almond-shaped eyes, filled with large black pupils, and their charming hint of being ever so slightly cross-eyed, added even more appeal, instantly creating in me a desire to look deep into them: into the softest black I had ever seen, that contained not the slightest hint of the evil so often associated with the colour.

I think each of us was fascinated to be able to study and delight in a similar creature from a different set of genes, one that produced something very pleasing to the other's senses. Unfortunately this mutual admiration went on for probably no more than two or three minutes before my grandfather's booming voice summoned me back to the house.

I was loath to leave her, something inside was anchoring me to the spot. My upbringing, however, had taught me not to keep adults waiting. So I went, not without sorrow and not without wishing to know how another few minutes would have affected the strange new feelings that I carried away.

The next day, Grandfather had decided, should be one of rest. He retired to the bar — he told me, to catch up with fellow travellers from home, something I later learned had not been the sole attraction — and I adjourned to the garden, mindful to stay within sight of the other guests enjoying its delights. I was engrossed in some book and enjoying the friendly air when I heard a voice.

It was an impressive deep voice, rich in tone and abundantly endowed with sincerity. When I looked up I could only see a silhouette in front of the burning sun. I shielded my eyes and focused on a pair of white trousers.

"How are you enjoying Raffles?" asked the voice from above them.

When I realised it was the stranger from the front door I leapt to my feet. By changing the angle I could see him clearly. He was again dressed all in white. His eyes contained the same interest and benevolence. His voice had already identified him as an Englishman. I guessed his age to be the same as an elderly father or a young grandfather, and made a note in my diary that now attests to the truth of the youthful description that follows.

"May I join you?" he asked, moving to the part of the bench closest to him and sitting before I had the presence of mind to reply. He looked at me with a smile, a more permanent relation of the fleeting one I had seen on the day we arrived.

I sat down, not knowing what to say but strangely pleased he had sought me out. My shyness was not a problem he shared. "How are you enjoying Raffles?" he asked again.

"I think it's wonderful sir," I blurted out with boyish enthusiasm.

"So do I. So do I." He smiled, accepting my remark and sharing the excitement with which I'd offered it, apparently pleased with my answer. "Do you understand why?"

I looked at him. I had been taught to conceal my emotions and answer questions factually, in a manner befitting the occasion, with the appropriate words. Explaining one's feelings was totally superfluous. Conversation was an art that had to be learned. The higher one's station in life, the more seriously the subject was to be taken. If fault were to be found with an answer I believed, on most occasions, that it could be attributed to allowing the inappropriate emotion, usually excitement or — as I was to learn later — lust, to override the words that discipline dictated should be chosen adequately to demonstrate one's intelligence and breeding.

Still, watching him, looking into the expectant eyes, it was obvious he had asked seriously and was waiting for me to reply. He hoped, I knew, for something more intuitive than "It's warm and I might see a tiger attack someone" — particularly as I had already answered the first question with insufficient preparation and inadequate aplomb. So, not wanting to say anything that he might interpret as ignorance on my part, I settled on some simple words that would, I trusted, not be deemed inappropriate or dim-witted and might prompt him to supply a more detailed explanation; for I honestly had not the slightest inkling why I enjoyed the hotel. I had been far too busy enjoying myself to analyse anything. "No sir, I don't believe I do. I think it's partly the difference from everything I've known before."

He gave me a smile: I'm happy to say, an understanding one. I think he knew I didn't want to disappoint him. I'm also sure he was aware that I didn't really know.

"Raffles stands for all the fables of the exotic East," he said, very graciously, "that you unwittingly are being exposed to."

'Exotic' struck a chord in me. It was a word I would not have thought of but, yes, exotic was very appropriate. The Chinese girl in the garden, with the enchanting face, had certainly been exotic. As was the thought of a tiger roaming and looking for someone to eat; or equally, of a man creeping through the jungle, his senses razor sharp, on the alert for one's presence. Even this man in the white suit was himself exotic, in a very refined way.

When I left my thoughts and returned my gaze to him he was studying me, remaining silent so as not to interrupt. Perhaps he had been sharing my thoughts with me. If he had told me he had been I should not have been surprised.

"It is the blend. For most people, their own culture holds no particular fascination. The real intrigue comes when the colour of one is blended with another. The more one mixes, the more fascinating things one sees. When the faithful Christian is confronted with the devout Buddhist, a question he has not thought of before is raised. Those who measure the worth of a hostess by the silver mark on her cutlery have their values questioned when confronted with the stark practicality of chopsticks. Societies that cosset women, condemning them to unfulfilling roles, must wonder why when their Asian counterparts perform manual labour without sacrificing their femininity or elegance. It is the differences that highlight the contrast and create the exotic.

"Raffles began as a transposed piece of Europe. The intention, however, could not keep out the cultures surrounding it. Nor, wisely, did it want to; it is far richer for having welcomed them, embraced them warmly. Now it is neither European nor Asian."

"Then how would you describe it sir?"

"It should not matter to you in the least how I would describe it. Your image is the only one that is important. I should have no difficulty in relaying its allure to people who have never been here. I certainly can't describe it to you. You already have your own perception, even if it has not yet completely developed. When you're on the ship sailing for home it will come to you, you will find the words, and you will use them to tell your friends and relatives. And what you tell them will be no less fascinating or accurate than my words to those willing to listen to me."

I looked into his face without saying a word. At the time I was unaware this conversation would remain with me for so many years; or that what he was teaching me would enrich each one of them.

"Look around you," he said, continuing my instruction.

I did, with great interest. I looked at the rich green of the garden, noticing the tranquillity of white coated men — with trays bearing seductive long glasses of red liquid and shorter ones that could be mistaken for water by everyone but the English — walking silently across manicured lawns to guests who had sought out the shaded areas.

There was a sound of contentment that I had never heard before. If asked to describe it I could only have said it was the sound of the breeze on grass and the flowers responding to the sun. It was the only visual sound I have ever encountered. This meaningful silence I only found at Raffles — and as easily on subsequent trips as on the first. It was a joy I wouldn't have discovered without my new friend.

"Do you think the East lives under a different sun?"

A strange question, but I found it worthy of consideration. I was too polite not to. I looked around. I looked up. There was no denying that the effect of the sun was different in these unfamiliar surroundings, knocking guests off their feet with its intensity, ensuring nights full of gay activity by the same people, transformed from victims to beneficiaries, with stored and renewed energy.

Even the sanctity of the building couldn't repel the sunlight's invasion; however, everything was created to ensure that its presence was welcomed and suitably celebrated. Cool colonial rooms provided excellent views as it played in the tropical gardens; and magnificent windows transformed its rays to fascinating live pictures, adorning interior walls.

Again I had seen something new, though I had been in this garden every day since my arrival.

"You've travelled widely in Asia?" I inquired — thinking he had perhaps spent time studying under a mystic or miraculous guru, who had opened his eyes to so many things that others just walked blindly past.

"Yes, though most of my discoveries have been made here."

I looked suitably perplexed by his statement. How could he have discovered Asia here, I asked myself.

"Look," he said, interrupting my thoughts.

Walking around the boundary of the garden was a man dressed in a way I had never seen. He wore flowing orange robes that stood out from the sober white wall he passed, his grey shadow merging into it as though to apologise, an emissary seeking peace. The robe flew and ran with the gentlest breeze, demonstrating an exquisite quality. That he was nevertheless fully covered meant he had endless layers surrounding him.

Above the finery was a modest head; the hair shaved to a fine, even stubble. The brown skin, like his expression, seemed soft and contemplative. His mind, I'm sure, was elsewhere.

I looked at the man in white. He was watching with understanding and admiration. He made no comment. None was necessary. It was obvious, even to my inexperienced eyes, that the man was possessed by a peace that came from within and was greater than any I would ever know. The brightness of his garment reflected not his character but his position in a hierarchy of which I knew nothing.

"And there," said the man in white, knowing I had answered the first puzzle for myself.

I forgot the monk as I focused on a European of considerable proportions. He wore a monocle between a wide-brimmed hat and a handlebar moustache that covered a small tight mouth. His girth, contrasted with the slim Asians who followed him, was a sad example of European excess. In the expressionless faces of the men trailing him I sensed a hidden smile, a desire to laugh.

The heavy European stopped abruptly. The line behind him condensed like an accordion on the downstroke. The monocle sent back the sun's inquisitive rays as the large head turned frantically on its thick stump of a neck. Then, seeing — or not finding — what he sought, his short legs started again as quickly as they had come to rest. The followers extended like the accordion on the up-stroke and the procession moved unhappily on.

"Peace, and turmoil," said the man in white.

His eyes had moved on, scouring the surrounds, searching for another mystery. At the far end of the garden he found it. There was a small break in the greenery and a tiny brown figure crouched there peering through it. Little fingers invaded the fence on each side of a thin face. The whites of the eyes and his teeth were apparent even from our distance.

I glanced at my friend, who studied the face as though the boy were two feet away. He appeared to be Indian. He watched the goings on in the strange world with an impassive face, devoid of envy or anger. If there was any surprise, it too was not showing. He watched, it seemed, purely because there was a gap in the hedge and, momentarily, the new scene held his attention over the more familiar sights surrounding him outside. The tiny hands grasping the wire were his link to the inside, a link that was totally in his control, the only kind he wanted.

The eyes of the man in white had found a woman at the opposite end of the garden to the urchin. For a moment I wondered if she might be his wife. She also was dressed in white, and was seated in the shade, casually resting with her dress immaculately laid out around her; even while she reclined, its excellent tailoring was obvious. Dark hair fell from beneath the white hat; and a hand, holding a tiny handkerchief, dabbed her eyes.

"If you go home and tell your friends you sat in the garden with a stranger and saw a little Indian boy looking through the fence, a monk meditating, an irritated foreigner and a crying woman it would be a simple truth. And a wasted journey.

"Imagine, however, that what we are really looking at is far less obvious than we think and far more sinister. Always remember, my young friend, that where we have no excitement we must create it. And where we can't recognise it we must learn to."

He looked at me. I at him. To me the simple scene he had first described was the one I surely would have carried home and recalled; at least, until the bland honesty of it had forced me to replace it with more interesting events.

"The woman arrived in Singapore," he began, closing his eyes briefly as if to see his vision more clearly, "from Eastern Europe with the heavy gentleman, to whom she has the misfortune to be married. He is a former army officer, who had been more concerned with how he looked in his uniform than what it represented. His wife, who has grown to hate him for his brutality and lack of consideration, had her disenchantment crystallised on the long sea journey here aboard a British steamer.

"The fine manners and attention of the officers re-introduced her to the ways in which gentlemen are supposed to behave; and her unhappiness with her husband, whose conduct grew worse as his jealousy increased, became more than she could bear.

"It led to an argument in the cabin one night. He beat her mercilessly, and required her to stay below deck for five days, until the bruises and lacerations had healed. When she emerged, the officers were less attentive — for her safety — and the final part of the trip was the longest, an icy presence on the tepid sea.

"Once ashore she only stayed with him for two days; then, sensing her chance to escape, she fled." He paused, searching for the monk. The quiet man obliged by appearing near the woman in the shade, as if obeying my mysterious friend's mental instruction.

"She walked to and fro among the streets, alone, with one small bag, which was all she could carry, less afraid of the strange surroundings and alien sights than she was of the man she was fleeing from. In need more of compassion than help, she entered a temple. The monk befriended her. At first she was wary of the gentle man in the orange clothes. To her, being unskilled in the ways of the world and unfamiliar with its fascinating differences, he was merely a man in a strange robe, not a man amongst men.

"However, his tranquillity won her confidence and renewed her strength. After she had recounted her story she discovered how deeply understanding he was. He gave her shelter and the sympathy she had not known for so long. It allowed her to cleanse her soul of the unhappiness she had kept inside, that had begun to poison her own kindness of heart. In the process his robes lost their strangeness and he became her symbol of renewed hope and salvation. Her rescuer.

"He had saved her and directed her first tentative steps along the road to recovery. It was a blessing for her; for him it was simply one more episode in a lifetime devoted to others. Soon a well-to-do Chinese businessman, a Buddhist, brought her here knowing she'd be safe and would have the solitude to think about her future in a more familiar setting. The monk, however, stayed close by in case of need. He will not leave her until he knows she is in no more emotional or spiritual danger."

"And the boy?" I asked anxiously, fascinated by his tale, and looking back at the fence, seeing the tiny hands and white dots still peering through.

"The boy acted as the spy, finding the woman and reporting her location to her husband. Sadly, he is wise beyond his years. A desperate little fellow who will do anything for the little it takes to blind his conscience to his deeds. In this instance the same minute sum that the European had offered to every street urchin he encountered, certain that one of them would produce a return on his investment.

"This despite the infatuation the boy feels for her. You see, once they came face to face in the street he was charmed by the kindness in her eyes and warmed by a smile that captivated him.

"However, sadly for our heroine, his family's need of the pittance the cruel man had offered ensured that he would report her whereabouts, even though he felt disgust at doing so. He sensed from the start how evil the husband was. The boy shares the dens of renegades and thieves; he therefore had no difficulty in identifying the European's character the moment he saw him.

"The fat man's search though, will be unsuccessful. His rage and insensitivity blind him to his wife's newfound peace and understanding. The woman he is looking for, that he had created, no longer exists.

"Now the urchin is on a different mission. The clenched fists and whites in the eye are caused by his concern for the woman. He watches to see what will happen. If she is harmed he knows people who will help him seek revenge. It will cost him nothing and the bullying husband will be hurt beyond belief by the scoundrels the boy will call, who have an instinctive urge to spill blood."

"Oh please," I cried, not wanting to see the woman hurt, "could you not be mistaken?"

"Of course I could," he said with an absent smile, "I should be very surprised if *their* truth had the slightest thing in common with mine. You see, I'm telling you there is often more to see than appears to be there. And whatever it is that you discern is your truth. Theirs probably doesn't even interest them; if there were any way to divest themselves of it I have no doubt they would. Unable to, as they are, I dare say they have not the least interest in how things will turn out."

As you can imagine this conversation was deserving of more than a twelve-year-old mind, the owner of which would have been content to pass the afternoon enjoying the sunshine and a book, oblivious to the fat man's quest, the monk's concern, the urchin's shame and the woman's despair. In fact, I'm sure none of them would have received more than a cursory glance — and the boy peering through the fence would not have been spotted at all, even during one of the breaks I always rewarded myself with at the end of a chapter.

That evening I joined my grandfather for dinner in the Elizabethan Grill. Knowing him to be a worldly man and as wise as any I had yet met, I felt it would be prudent to find out if the extraordinary things I had been told were ideals I should pursue, or purely idle holiday chatter, an unkind form of teasing practised only on those too young and polite to recognise it as such, by people with nothing better to do. Though I hardly felt it was the latter, I included the possibility in my thoughts merely to offer an alternative — as I'd been told all discussions should have at least two points of view.

After a few days of tropical weather, and strange food that, I'm ashamed to say, was a little too 'unusual' for my immature palate, and streets teeming with foreigners — it was pleasing, if somewhat unadventurous, to see the silver trolley approach and, with great ceremony, have its top rolled back to reveal a familiar and welcome sight: roast beef and Yorkshire pudding.

We spoke little before the meal was served and even less when the various courses were laid before us, preferring to enjoy the service that spoiled us by creating expectations we should find extremely hard to fulfil when we returned home — for me impossible, as I would return to the austerities of my boarding school.

Finally, when the table was cleared and my grandfather had exchanged his empty Burgundy bottle for a port and a large cigar, I told him about my meeting with the man in white. He seemed proud that an adult should spend his precious time at Raffles with a grandson of my age, and muttered something about good education never being wasted. I, of course, did not tell him the afternoon had had a distinct student-teacher flavour to it; rather I let the proud thoughts of his grandson's maturity run their course.

"Grandfather," I began tentatively, when his musing was complete, "how important is truth?"

"Paramount," he said vehemently, having given the answer not a moment's contemplation; and immediately lifted his head, blowing smoke cartwheeling towards the ceiling.

I obviously hadn't phrased the question correctly. I had learned very early in life the virtue of telling the truth and, perhaps even more importantly, the absolute necessity of owning up promptly to one's indiscretions.

"Perhaps I didn't mean truth, grandfather. That gentleman over there," I said, pointing as discreetly as I could to ensure my grandfather focused on the correct one of a dozen men who were, like him, lifting their heads above their port filled hands and contributing to a thin swirling layer of fog hovering just below the ceiling.

"An English businessman," he said with supreme confidence, after a very summary glance.

"And if I suggested he was a pirate captain on vacation, what would you say?"

"I'd say you were wrong," he said with a wry smile, "I met him this afternoon in the bar. He's an English businessman. He's here buying copra. I offered to introduce him to the you know, what's-their-name's, that we visited yesterday."

I looked hard and long into my lime juice. The benefit of my afternoon's experience seemed to be coming undone. But I tried again, convinced there was great enlightenment in the way the man in white had suggested I look at things. "Suppose two people guessed incorrectly. If one said he was a pirate on vacation and the other said a great white hunter from Africa, what would you think?"

He did not answer as quickly or as confidently this time. He contemplated the port and chewed the end of the cigar. "I imagine we're now entering the realm of story-telling."

"Is truth necessary for story-telling?" I asked, delighted that I had at least led him to stage two of the question instead of finding this new avenue to also be a dead end.

"If it were, your books would contain white pages between those elaborate covers," he said, chuckling with a Burgundy-and-port-induced gaiety.

"When I return home, should I tell my friends only the truth?"

"Good heavens no!" he said with a start, putting his glass down. "If you told them about our meal tonight they'd laugh and say why ever did you travel half-way around the world for roast beef and Yorkshire pudding? They should think us mad."

"So it is all right not to tell the truth, if it's..."

"My lad, when people back home have been unable to concentrate because of jealousy and longing to know what we're doing on our journey, it is our responsibility — nay, duty — to go back and justify their envy with tales of frightening originality and fascination."

I smiled. Obviously what the gentleman in white had said was not something my grandfather could not associate with. I decided not to press on any further. It had been hard enough to get the indirect blessing, that I interpreted his words to be. I should not risk having it countermanded by asking another inappropriate question. I was very pleased though when my grandfather kept the subject alive.

"Look around you. It will not be hard to recall fascinating tales. We are surrounded by them."

I did as grandfather asked; ashamed, after my afternoon's tuition, that I had not done so much earlier.

In the evening the scene surrounding us was, of

course, different from but no less exhilarating than those offered during the day. The room opened out onto the garden. Through the open doors I could see small circles of greenery illuminated below bamboo poles adorned with torches, lighting the way for guests wishing to take a stroll in the cool but humid night air. Mysterious silhouettes walked in all directions with unhurried anticipation. Some solitary men and women seemed to be playing strange games, pursuing but never catching, raising and lowering hats then moving on, partaking in a never-ending charade.

The popular songs of the day, delicately carved out of ivory, in some late night adult enclave that I had not seen, danced down the corridor and entered through the door on the opposite side of the room to the garden.

Only the occasional harsh car horn or the roar of loud voices, boisterous and intoxicated, passing by on the road outside, reminded us that we were not the world's sole survivors blessed for eternity in this lost island paradise.

Sadly, I have not aged as well as Raffles. While she is still so full of future my life holds many more memories than promises of new adventures. And recollections such as these have become my most treasured possessions, having taken on greater significance with the passing of time.

To me they highlight the greatest casualty of the scenes I have described — the lost elegance of humanity — something I cannot translate into words, but so important and enjoyable a part of life in the first half of this century. One of history's chief determinants, which once seemed ingrained in all men from birth. Today, it is so rare that Raffles and a handful of like-minded establishments fight vehemently to keep it from total extinction.

Last November I spent most of my time walking in the gardens and studying the marvellous structures above me, remembering kindly the special events and characters from previous visits. I am now quite content to find a comfortable spot in these familiar surroundings and enjoy my past; faithfully fulfilling my duty to keep friends, who have passed on, from being forgotten. Celebrating their contributions to life until I too am extinguished, at which time I shall remove their memories from this earth, hoping to share them again with their creator on the other side.

Grandson John, being older and more independent than I had been on my first trip, ventured further afield, no less fascinated than I had been with the differences of culture he had not been exposed to before.

One evening as we dined together he told me that he had met a girl, a Chinese girl; and asked if he could invite her for dinner the following night. Naturally I gave my blessing, although it would be our last evening at Raffles, as I looked forward to seeing whether he had inherited the faultless taste of his paternal grandfather…

The following day, for old times sake, I walked across to the waterfront. It required more effort than the same journey had in 1930. Singapore's progress had included the pushing back of the sea, and the view had been blocked, or enhanced, depending on your cast of mind, by a myriad ships. Tankers and freighters from all the ports of the world, sitting offshore, aligned by the tide in unison like a great floating ballet, waiting for their turn to unload their cargoes to feed the insatiable appetite of Singapore's thriving economy.

It was while looking at the same blue sea, watched by the ever smiling sky and assailed by the unrelenting sun, that I had had another, and, regrettably, last conversation with the man in white. I had seen him frequently during the days since our first chat in the garden, often meeting by chance in a corridor; he always managed, however, to impart some helpful words of wisdom, no matter how brief the encounter.

Only now, as I think back, do I realize that each time

we met I was alone. The one exception was the day when we arrived; and on that occasion, despite passing within touching distance, my grandfather appeared not to have noticed him. I had seen him several times, before entering the dining room and upon leaving it — even, once, on the way to the washroom. However, when I was with my grandfather he was never to be seen, not in the distance, not across the room, nor even on the far side of the compound — like his urchin or heroine. In fact such was his familiarity to me, and his non-existence to my grandfather, that I had been questioned seriously whether he did, in reality, exist. At the time I had no doubts that he did.

"What do you see?" asked the strong voice from behind me, anxious not to waste a precious minute with unnecessary greetings, when it could be better used to further my education.

I turned, having recognised the voice of the man in white before my eyes confirmed who it was. Other than showing a smile, to signal that his company was welcome and the panorama pleasing, I did not answer. My expression invited him to tell me.

"I have always loved the sea. Most passionately, when travelling across it bound for these shores," he said, looking past me, perhaps recalling some voyage worthy of special remembrance — though it would not have surprised me if, in his teeming mind, he felt they were all of special significance, worthy of frequent recollection. "This carpet of blue is being admired by black-skinned people in that direction," he said, pointing to my left, "and brown-skinned ones over there. It divides and unites mankind at the same time, instilling in all who stand on its border an irresistible desire to see what lies over the horizon. To encounter new cultures, and find new audiences for their own. Strangely this tiny island seems to lure the most interesting among those who take up the challenge."

He turned, leaning his back on the stone wall. "Apart from the opportunity it offers men like us, I don't support colonisation. It aims to convert and dilute, rather than admire and adapt or merge. It is a government's attempt to imitate zealous missionaries who go forth with the misguided assumption that all those they encounter have survived the centuries with inferior beliefs and ways of life.

"Can you imagine how people must have felt when strange white beings first appeared demanding that they live in unsuitable stone structures, wear clothes resembling a form of torture and swear allegiance to an unseen monarch when they were perfectly happy with what they already had? And all this while still trying to fathom the wisdom in the real missionaries' appeal to look forward to the immense joy of life after death?

"One day someone in a position of authority will realise there might be much to be learned from the people we are intent on making as dreary as the most tiresome amongst us. Pray that the value of their cultures will not have already been extinguished when it happens."

I turned, sharing the scene that held him. Foreign buildings sprouted from the green island. The streets were busy with motor cars and clanking trams; people walked this way and that. The Savile Row suits looked strange beside the coolies' white vests and the Sikhs' turbans. An occasional monk added a welcome shock of colour. Women sauntered under umbrellas that kept the sun off their fair skins but trapped the hot air around their coiffured hair and artificial faces.

"'East is East and West is West and never the twain small meet.' They meet all right, but blindly. Neither sees what the one offers the other. A sad waste that won't be remedied for a hundred years."

He looked at me seriously. His face wore an unfamiliar sombre expression. "I want you to promise that you will remember this scene as it is today. I want you to recognise two indifferent cultures, each as intent as the other on rejecting change and refusing compromise. I want you to remain aware of the exotic and always treasure it. I want you to travel in Asia and note the differences, savour and benefit from everything you learn. Enrich yourself and your life. I want you to do it there." He tilted his head towards the white landmark that stood in front of us.

"Raffles Hotel is above colonialism. I dare say, and I regret I shall not be here to see it, that it will also survive the assault of the passing years and the deadly uniformity so-called progress relies on. It shall, I'll venture, graciously adopt only what is necessary to ensure that the guests of the future find it as intriguing as we do today. And gracefully decline the future's more common and unsuitable traits. It will, however, retain its attraction for things exotic and the people who treasure them. No matter how sterile the world becomes, it will not contaminate that building. Raffles will change at its own pace; and people looking for things that no longer exist elsewhere will always be able to find them there.

"I have no doubt that, if not in your lifetime then certainly within your children's, you'll see a revolution as the patience and tolerance of these kindly hardworking people will one day be repaid manifold. This scene will be improved, it will be the closest thing to a miracle a mortal will ever see, as more intelligent beings appreciate and blend the best of both worlds. That is why you must remember this, and rejoice in what will replace it."

As he walked away I watched him go, growing smaller and smaller, and reflected on all that he had said. His wisdom seemed endless; his observations profound.

When he reached the top step he stopped and turned around to face me. He raised his arm and waved it gently. I waved to him. Then he turned again and seemed to disappear into the white building.

I looked at the blue sky; he had during one of our discussions referred to it as the witness. I smiled at its infinity and beauty, thinking of the effect it had on emotions and the perspective it put on one's own importance. It had heard what was said that day in 1930 and was contributing the energy required for it to come true.

I came back to the present. The ships seemed to have increased in number during my brief mental absence. As I turned, the scene was vastly different, with the exception of an aspect of Raffles. The white building was still prominent, though dwarfed by giant structures, built with the soulless uniformity that the man in white had predicted.

I had thought of his farewell many times. Over the years it had taken on a mystical significance. When he had lowered his arm and disappeared into the hotel it was, literally, as though he had turned into the hotel; a merging of like souls, white into white, white with white, purity and sanctity, imagination with reality. It is perhaps a ridiculous thought though, strangely, it has grown more vivid as I have grown older. Now, although at a time of life when the proximity of death adds a frightening significance to every new day, I do not find it hard to believe. The man in white could well have been the spirit, the embodiment, of the grand white edifice. Explaining to me mysteries that would otherwise have remained unresolved.

I took my thoughts and went back into the embrace of his beloved Raffles, to prepare myself for dinner. The young lady was due in slightly over an hour.

When she walked into the bar with John I recognised her immediately. She was my girl from the garden. Though modern and obviously well educated, she smiled with the same ageless charm. Her face was olive, surrounded by thick black hair that shared her skin's vitality and perfection. She had the same fascinating slightly almond eyes, in the same friendly shade of black. She spoke with the energy of her race and brought delight to an evening that such generously endowed beings were created to enhance.

I rediscovered the feelings I had known in 1930. They weren't of course the strange unknown sensations that they had been, but they were no less exciting. I was glad to know that my girl could still appeal to a mature me. It was something I had wondered about often.

Needless to say we all enjoyed ourselves immensely. I was rejuvenated by her presence. But I felt a twinge of jealousy, and a touch of obsolescence, when John and Jade excused themselves and walked arm-in-arm into the garden. I knew the emotions John was feeling. I rejoiced that he had more time to revel in them than I had had.

I looked around, blew my cigar smoke towards the ceiling and raised my glass of port for a toast: "To wise men and exotic women." I glanced out of the doors at the young couple, secretly following their shadows, remembering all the others whom I had seen seduced by the garden through the years.

Asia has changed, just as my friend predicted it would. Independence has long since come to the proud and able people who had so graciously put up with interfering foreigners. With the changes it was inevitable that the cloak of mystery, that had for so long shrouded this faraway world, would be lifted. It has been replaced by open discussion of the all too practical and mundane things that concern modern men of all races. I believe now, more than ever, that Raffles does stand for the fables of the exotic East, being one of the very few places where they still exist. Where the contrasts are celebrated and revered.

I raised my eyes, recalling the face of the man who explained this wonderful mystery to me, knowing that, if he were anywhere, it would be here. Wondering whether, when the time comes, I might be fortunate enough to join him.

"To Raffles!" I said, lifting my glass again, unconcerned by the mirth my lone toasts were inspiring in neighbouring diners. "For proving beyond a doubt that East and West, despite the uninformed dictum, have always been destined to meet, for each is most exotic in the eye of the other; and without the deserved admiration their individual attractions would be sadly neglected.

"Finally, to all the people who have ensured Raffles a unique position — and with special gratitude to the man in white… Cheers, my dear friends. Until we meet again."

Tommy

JAN PRYOR

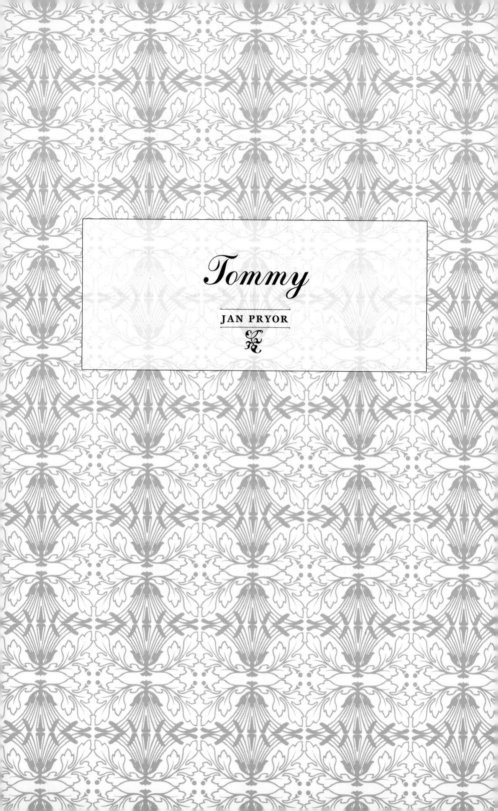

GENERALLY I am a lady of sober and conservative tastes.

However, some years ago I undertook an activity that raised eyebrows at the time and resulted in endless disapproval from my friends and acquaintances later. To be frank, even shoppers would turn to look at me in the street, barely hidden smiles dancing around the corners of their otherwise tight mouths. The most honest, of course, were the children, who would point openly at me and often laugh out loud.

The activity which ended with all this brouhaha started with a solitary holiday in Borneo. Now this may not sound like much to the world-weary traveller of today, but for a lady of middle years whose sense of adventure stopped at buying a new tea set in Orchard Road, it was indeed a storm in a teacup for my polite circle.

The fact of my going was enough to cause a ripple among my Singapore society friends. But the real shock came with the fellow who accompanied me on my return.

Without a word to my ruffled friends this total stranger, many years younger than I, moved into my home and made himself thoroughly comfortable.

We got on famously. Tommy was no bother at all and kept himself to himself, while acting as a most agreeable companion. I soon became used to seeing him thoughtfully chewing a piece of fruit as the sun came up behind the trees across the road. I didn't even mind sharing my secluded balcony with him — previously a favourite spot and out-of-bounds to visitors. It was a pleasure to see the soft morning light glint in his brown-gold hair and gently kiss the fine outline of his cheek.

I admit I was soon obsessed with my young friend. He responded with affection and we became almost inseparable.

A message was none-too-subtly delivered to my tea-party pals that if they requested the pleasure of my company then Tommy must be made welcome too.

It was too much. Several of my friends simply could not accustom themselves to this strange fellow who had appeared from deepest Borneo and apparently taken over my life. One or two even expressed concern about the safety of their silver should he visit. To this day I don't know whether their precious possessions are gathering dust in a bank vault, because I have never seen them again.

As the social butterflies moved away, Tommy and I grew even closer. There were only two places where I discouraged his company. One was the supermarket, where I feared his peace of mind would be upset with all the dither and din. The other was the zoo, which I visited occasionally with relatives who found Singapore a convenient staging post on their wider travels. Tommy, with his normal placid manner, had no comment when I explained the reasons for his exclusion and seemed content to stay at home by himself.

We lived this happy life for several years, settling into a gentle routine like an old married couple. Tommy was a warm and loving companion, although occasionally I saw a wistful look in his eye as the sun filtered through the trees bordering the Istana. He remained Borneo-born and I must confess in all honesty that I sometimes felt I did not know him well enough.

Then one dreadful day he simply disappeared.

As it happened, I had been to the zoo — alone, for the first time in months. As soon as I came home I felt the emptiness and knew my beloved Tommy was gone.

My distress was almost unbearable. I called and cried and frantically searched our favourite places for him. The loss was made even greater by the few things he left behind: his favourite chair, where the morning sun fell on an empty seat, the hand-knitted blanket he liked to keep near in case the night turned cool, the Royal Doulton plate from which he ate his breakfast fruit.

On Easter Monday 1993, a week after Tommy's disappearance, I went to the police. They listened politely enough, but as I left I heard their muffled laughter behind officially closed doors and I knew they thought me a foolish old woman.

There are few words to describe the loss of such a companion; the worst of it was not knowing why or where my precious friend had gone. I suffered many sleepless nights, imagining him lying in a drain, hit by a car, or wandering about the streets alone.

Gradually my courage and spirits began to mend. Three weeks after Tommy's departure I folded his blanket and put it away. His chair went back to its old place in the guest bedroom and his plate was returned to the pile on the pantry shelf. Somehow word spread through my old network that Tommy was gone and, with a certain kindness, my former friends invited me back into their embrace.

But nothing could replace my Tommy.

At the most inconvenient times I would remember

his slender body and brown face, crinkled up at some private joke. I compared his youthful suppleness to the hobbling gait of my regained friends, who moved like creaking old monuments; but such thoughts only reminded me of my own aging state.

One chum took me to Raffles for tea to fill in an empty afternoon. We enjoyed an elegant selection of cakes and lingered over the best Twinings tea, just as we had in the old days when such things mattered to me. As we left, we decided to renew our acquaintance with the Palm Court.

Resting for a moment on a shaded bench, I suddenly felt my host stiffen beside me. I turned to look at him and was aghast at the shock on his face.

"There's Tommy!"

He pointed towards the first floor suites of the hotel. My stomach lurched but I looked bravely anyway.

Sure enough, the cheeky monkey was there, swinging from a tree and chattering mischievously to himself. The long years of our association must have come back to him and he put on a fine show when he saw me. His twirling and shrieking drew staff and guests, who pointed and laughed with excitement. Then he blew me a farewell kiss — one of his favourite tricks — and disappeared over the balcony.

I was stunned.

My companion hugged me gently, took in the Hotel with a sweeping gesture, and said, "Well, you couldn't have lost him to a finer lady."

I see him mentioned often, although he has a new name now. Just the other day I picked up a glossy magazine for upper-end travellers, which explained how Martin the Monkey had first appeared before astonished guests at Raffles on the twenty-seventh of April 1993.

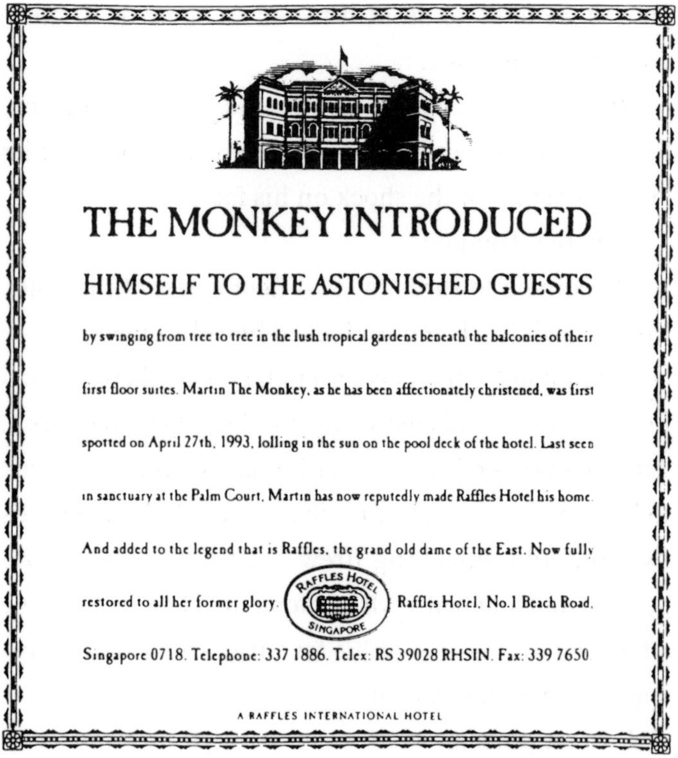
THE MONKEY INTRODUCED
HIMSELF TO THE ASTONISHED GUESTS
by swinging from tree to tree in the lush tropical gardens beneath the balconies of their first floor suites. Martin The Monkey, as he has been affectionately christened, was first spotted on April 27th, 1993, lolling in the sun on the pool deck of the hotel. Last seen in sanctuary at the Palm Court, Martin has now reputedly made Raffles Hotel his home. And added to the legend that is Raffles, the grand old dame of the East. Now fully restored to all her former glory.
RAFFLES HOTEL SINGAPORE
Raffles Hotel, No.1 Beach Road, Singapore 0718. Telephone: 337 1886. Telex: RS 39028 RHSIN. Fax: 339 7650
A RAFFLES INTERNATIONAL HOTEL

Actually, he is an orang-utan, and was saying goodbye to me; but who am I to ruin the latest fable to grow up around that great hotel?

The White-beaded Dress

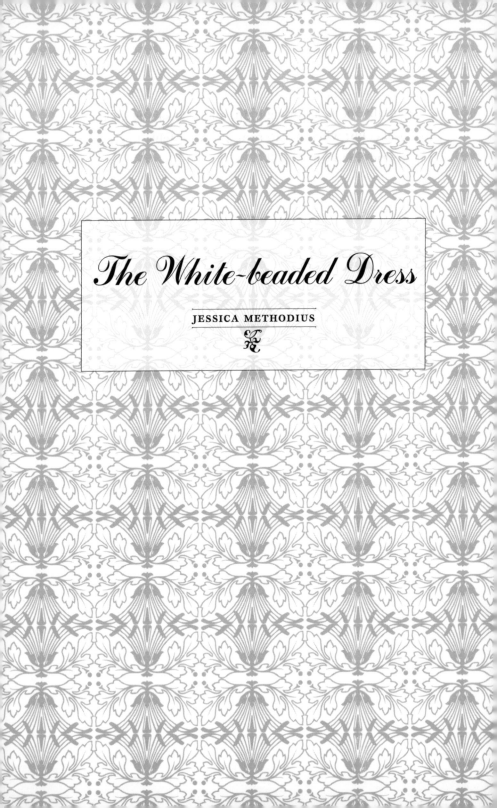

JESSICA METHODIUS

IT'S Saturday again. I can feel the morning sunlight on my face through the parting of my window curtains. Another day, another weekend. To tell you the truth, I feel rather bored with my life. What life does a seventeen-year-old have, anyway, in a sterile city? Study, go shopping, play basketball, go to the movies, sneak into a pub once in a way? Nothing exciting ever happens to me. I guess it's because I live in such unexciting times. After all, everything's been done already. The moon has been explored, the Wall's down, there's no more mystique about royalty, anybody can be a pop star or an actor, and everyone seems to want economic progress. I believe those are the two dullest, most unimaginative words in the English language.

"Karen!"

There goes my mum. She thinks I'm just too lazy to get up. She doesn't seem to realise that mornings are my most philosophically prolific periods.

"Karen, it's time you were up."

She seems to think it's a national tragedy if I'm not up by eight o'clock. Mum thinks I'm not normal either. She thinks I don't spend enough time doing things normal teenagers should be doing. I guess she's right. I think life now is lacklustre. No romance in it. And I don't mean romance in a lovey-dovey sort of way like some jerks out there are bound to think. No, what I'm talking about is a certain quality of life and style that people of a bygone era used to have, like Mabel. She's my grandmother, by the way, and another thorn in my mum's flesh. What I mean is that my grandmother and people of her generation lived life in a time when things were happening, when Singapore was considered exotic and manners were refined and defined. I get all dreamy and wide-eyed when she tells me stories from her youth. Of course she's more than ninety now but she's not senile or anything like that. She's got far too much sense to let her brains go to putty. She's my favourite person in the world. Everyone else is rather afraid of her. They think she's eccentric. Even Mum. Perhaps it's because she doesn't tolerate fools easily, or boring people. If you don't come up to my grandmother's standards as a person, you'll know sooner or later. Often it is sooner.

Mabel though is unique, still very lucid, always voluble. She used to go to the Raffles a lot when she was a young woman back in the twenties. It must have been quite a sight then. I know it's been refurbished and all. Incidentally, that's another word I hate. Refurbished; also renovated, redecorated and retrofitted. Puerile words. I wish they'd just use 'done up'. After all the Raffles is a grand old lady. She should indeed have been done up. Anyway, coming back to it, I kind of wish I'd been there before they'd done anything to the Raffles. I can't help having this crazy notion that I might have come across one of Kipling's thumbprints on the wall, or discovered a strand of Ava Gardner's hair stuck beneath a floorboard. It must have been marvellous in my grandmother's time. I wish I had been there in the twenties, just to have one breathtaking tour around the rooms, gulp the same air as Coward or Maugham and take a peek at one of the grand balls they used to hold. I guess that's what my mum means by not being normal. She'd rather I went gaga over Rick Price than about a way of life that's in the past. I haven't lost touch with reality though, and I think that proves I'm normal. There's a certain wisdom in all the things my grandmother says to me. What I find refreshing about Mabel is that she is so unlike other old people. She tells things like they were, without mourning old ways or condemning new ones. She's always telling me for instance to never regret the choices I make in life. I haven't so far.

I think I'll go visit her today. My junior college is holding a prom cum fancy dress contest to mark the end of the school term. I don't normally go to stuff like that. I'd sooner stay home and read a good book. This time however, the theme seems rather fun: 'A blast from the past.' It's the only chance I'll get of acting out my fantasies. Know what I thought of going as? A flapper, with my hair in marcel waves, sangria-red lips and nails, and ostrich feathers. I'll try to cadge a dress off Mabel.

My grandmother incidentally lives fifteen minutes away from my family's condominium, with my eldest uncle's family. The fact that she lives there is coincidence and not a tradition. She merely chose to live with the only member of her family who owned a bungalow. She's very English in her ways. A female WOG. My grandmother is quite a character. She was the eldest daughter in a rich Hokkien family. Her father owned rubber plantations in Skudai and was quite liberal for a man of his generation. He made sure all his children, sons and daughters, had a good education.

Mabel studied at the convent in Victoria Street. She was fairly headstrong, insisting on earning her keep after her studies instead of waiting at home to be "auctioned off to the highest bidder," as she puts it. She secured a position as secretary to an English businessman who had an office at Collyer Quay. She was only seventeen then. My age. She probably got the job because she was that rare bird, a Chinese girl who was educated and spoke perfect English. She was also very pretty, terribly petite with a perfect oval face and hazel eyes that even now sparkle from the sockets in her wrinkled face. I guess that's why John Harrison, her employer, fell for her. I think he was from Liverpool, judging by the way Mabel still says "Pick that up luv" with a Scouse accent.

My family is rather tight-lipped about the whole affair. It's kind of unmentionable stuff, condemned to lie forever in the Lim family hall of shame. I don't know why they want respectability so badly. I think it's a great privilege to have a black sheep in the family, especially an adulterous black sheep. It's sort of comforting and inspirational to know that someone in the bloodline has had the courage to break out of the mould of a safe, mundane existence. I wouldn't even call that a life. At least one is reassured that one's heritage has been remarkable. I had a friend in primary school whose grandfather had been a notorious con man in the early fifties. I thought that was fascinating, but obviously she didn't think so and tried to camouflage the fact.

You have to be very careful with my grandmother. She doesn't like anything that reminds her of her Chinese roots. I saw her once literally screech abuse at a kindly lady who tried to help her across the road but who made the unforgivable mistake of calling her "Ah So". I have to call her "Mabel" boldly like I would a friend, not "Ah Mah", as all my friends call their grandmothers.

As I enter my uncle's house, greet my aunt and make my way into Grandma's room, I can't help but think again how unique and refreshing she is. So totally unlike the image in the sepia photograph on the wall, yet lacking none of the character or vibrancy displayed in the pretty, sparkling eyes more than half a century ago. My grandmother's room, where she spends most of her time these days, is spacious and papered with delicate gold sprigs. There are lots of comfortable cushions thrown about for visitors to sit on. On the far wall across her bed, hangs a blown-up newspaper photograph of the late Shirin Fozdar, Singapore's premier women's activist. Elsewhere, Art Deco prints hang on the walls, together with a copy of one of Gauguin's Tahiti paintings. Her bookshelves cover another wall. Hardy, the Brontes and Jane Austen; jacket to jacket with Dinesen, Waugh and Ruth Rendell. When she dies, she says she'll bequeath them all to me.

There she is — a tiny figure reclining on her sofa. She should be wearing a samfoo or one of those modified samfoo trouser-blouse outfits other Chinese old ladies wear. Not my grandmother. She is wearing a diaphanous nightgown with spaghetti straps and a plunging V neckline that displays her crêpy neck and accentuates her shrivelled breasts. Why is it that pretty girls turn into such ugly old women? So, there she is: ninety-two years old, the garish red hollow of her old lips around a cigarette, her gnarled fingers with nails painstakingly painted blood-red by Elvira the maid.

Mei Yuen, my grandmother's fifteen-year-old bitch, barks in welcome.

"Hi Mabel, how are you?" I say.

She looks at me, and motions me to sit down. She reminds me of a Russian diva. She must have observed and imbibed these mannerisms during the years she rubbed shoulders with the colonial expatriates.

"I've got a party next week, a fancy-dress party. I was thinking of going as a flapper. Do you think I could borrow your white-beaded dress?" I ask. I believe in coming to the point.

Her eyes go filmy. She slowly, almost painfully, closes them.

"The beaded dress," she mouths almost silently.

"I've only worn that dress once in my life."

"At the Raffles." She needs only this one prompt from me.

She shuts her eyes, then suddenly whispers, "'Raffles stands for all the fables of the exotic East' Somerset Maugham. It's strange, you know, how the East always seems exotic to Westerners when they are propped up on a deck chair in a very modern hotel writing their diaries.

"I am quite sure Sir Stamford Raffles wouldn't have used that term when he first set eyes on Singapore. Wild, unknown, uncivilised, yes; exotic, no.

"The allure was heightened when you had a marked contrast. The English bungalows, dinner parties, old copies of *The Times*, the ladies in their flowered cotton dresses, a bit of old England. And, just across the road, colourful Singapore: Tamil coolies, Chinese opium dens, Malay kampungs, girls in sarongs.

"I'm sure the Raffles is legendary for the same reasons. A bit of the Dorchester in exotic Singapore. I first visited the Raffles in 1921.

"John Harrison, my English boss and lover, had asked me to go with him to a party, at the Raffles: my first party. I was so thrilled." Even now, her face lights up as she says this.

"We had known each other for about two years. Of

course he never brought me home and never suggested anything to indicate that ours would be a long-term relationship. Our meetings weren't clandestine — to say the least — however. He didn't take pains to conceal our affair. I was well known to his friends and colleagues as his mistress. He would put his arm around me in public — when we were invited to dinner by other couples, or at Shakespeare plays organised by the expatriate women.

"He said I was unlike any of the other local girls. He could talk to me, and I would understand him."

She sighs and continues, "We could discuss Lloyd George and Art Nouveau, Dickens and colonial politics, all in the same breath. I thought the world of him, and that no local could be like him or live up to my expectations.

"I had always told my father that I did not want to live as the wife of a Hokkien tycoon, tolerating his seven mistresses and seventeen illegitimate children, and praying that my first-born child would be a boy to please my husband.

"With John, I could be the person I wanted to be, uninhibited, intellectual, independent and free from tradition.

"It was a few weeks before the party that I noticed subtle changes in him. He was edgy, unfocused — as we would say now — and moody."

Mabel pauses and swallows painfully before she continues, "On a few occasions, I had seen John furtively talking to a young Chinese girl outside the office. When I enquired who that was, he offhandedly answered, 'Oh one of the lower classes looking for a free ride.'

"I was too engrossed in preparing for my first party at the Raffles to be suspicious. The party was to be held for Guy Markham, a young official in the service who was being posted back to England. I knew him as one of John's best friends. He had requested the posting because his wife Olive had pestered him to do so, finding the tropical heat appalling and the colonial life oppressive. I had of course considered the possibility that John's moodiness could stem from the thought that he would miss his friend. But what of it? He had me didn't he?

"I was tremendously excited about the party. Besides myself, only a few locals would be present.

"I had the white-beaded dress especially tailored for me at a shop in Beach Road. Funnily enough, it was John who had shown me a photograph of it in a six-month-old copy of *The Tatler*. A young debutante was wearing it to one of the balls of the London season of 1920.

"'It'll look gorgeous on you,' he had said.

"And so of course I ordered flowy white chiffon and real imported Venetian glass beads, at great cost. The beads were painstakingly stitched on, one by one, by my tailor. With the dress, I was going to wear the pearl choker and tear-drop earrings my uncle had brought back with him from a trip to Japan.

"As the day of the party approached, John's tetchiness increased. It was almost as if he were pining for something.

"Once, when I was slow in taking down some dictation for him, he lost his temper and called me a stupid bitch, something he had never done in our two years together.

"I valiantly hoped the party at the Raffles — with the certainty of good food and music — would restore some of his humour.

"He let me off work at about three o'clock in the afternoon, to have time to prepare myself.

"I had my bath, and soaked in Yardley lavender bath salts. Ah Ling, my old amah, took ages to do my hair, mostly because I kept asking her to redo it. Finally, it was done. I still had long hair then. I don't think the shingled look had caught on in the East yet. There I was, my hair elegantly coiled behind my neck. I put on the dress.

“A beautiful fit. I had much the same figure as you now, my dear.

“Finally, I slicked on my ruby red lipstick, and then I was ready for John to take me to the Raffles.

“We arrived there at about six-thirty. It was really magical. He asked me to sit out in the garden first while he went off for some purpose. The night air was balmy with the fragrance of the grass and trees. I was sitting on a rattan chair, sipping a gin and tonic. My first drink. Me a local girl, at the Raffles Hotel. It was beautiful: the warm glowing light from the chandeliers of the ballroom within; and the sounds of Charleston music, tinkling champagne glasses and clipped English accents outside.

“I was drunk with the pleasure of that scene. It is something I always remember — even now, and especially when I feel depressed — as clearly as a still from a movie.”

She looks at me and says, “After all, Karen, what is life without memories?”

She resumes her story. “I was awed but, while enjoying the mood, I had noticed through the corner of my eye the Chinese girl from the office, loitering outside. I wondered what she was doing at the Raffles. She didn’t look like an invited guest, dressed in her plain samfoo with her hair tied severely behind her head.

"Just then, John came out. 'The guests of honour will be arriving soon,' he said. 'Time we went in.'

"He pulled me into the ballroom and navigated me right to the front so quickly that all I had was a whirlwind impression of sequins, smoke and laughter. Then there was a hush, as someone announced 'Guy and Olive'. Standing at the front, John and I were visible to all the crowd behind us. I gasped as I saw Olive. She was wearing the same dress as me, right down to the white crêpe rosette fastened at the back. She looked aghast — and then outraged.

"'What's this John?', she managed to choke out. 'Why is she wearing this? You told me I would look good in it. Why are you humiliating me like this?'"

"'That's right you bitch,' John snarled, now a total stranger to me. 'You deserve to be humiliated.'

"The rest of the events that night were a blur," Mabel says. "There was shouting and confusion. The girl in the samfoo, apparently Olive's maid, was asking John for her payment for helping to persuade her mistress to wear the same white dress — from the magazine — to the party.

"Amidst all this, I don't know how I came to find myself sitting outside, my head in my hands, dazed.

"'So it's finally out then?' said a voice in my ear.

"I looked up to see one of our acquaintances, a British official who had always been friendly towards me, although he always appeared to be just a little inebriated.

"'What do you mean?' I asked, dumbfounded.

"'Had to happen sooner or later, his cracking up like that at the thought of them leaving for good.'

"'You mean, John and Olive…'

"'No, I mean John and his fancy boy. Good God! You really don't know, do you?

"'Worst thing in the world to happen to a man like him. They've been close since they were in school. Too close for many, I dare say. His link with his past, Guy was. When Guy joined the service and was assigned here, Harrison naturally followed. They've hunted together, played and eaten together regularly for twenty-odd years. Never more than a day away from each other. The highlight of their week was a bridge game here at the Raffles followed by an evening at the Long Bar. He's going to miss all that. He's going to lose the companionship — and the intimacy — and he can't take it. That's why he's cracked up and taken it all out on Olive — who I'm sure was blissfully unaware of the intensity of her husband's relationship with your Harrison.'"

My grandmother's deep raspy voice continues, "You see Karen, people everywhere want their money's worth. Harrison wanted a genuine local girl — traditionally thought of as having less emotional depth than a Western woman. And he used me to the hilt. To serve him, when he needed physical comfort; to provide him with a kind of respectability; and ultimately to humiliate the woman who was taking his lifeline away.

"And I too had wanted my money's worth, believing him to be the genuine article, the perfect English gentleman with a bowler hat, who would give me a life of comfort, culture and kindness."

Grandma snorts, "You know, if he hadn't been in the East, with all its allure, exoticism and privilege, I quite believe he would have ended up being a dockhand in Liverpool.

"I believe I came out stronger from that whole experience. I realised I was a 'banana' — or, if you prefer, a Westernised Oriental Gentlewoman — and I liked being that way, in spite of Harrison. I lived my life the way I wanted for nearly three-quarters of a century now and I've no regrets.

"People everywhere are the same, Karen. Why do you think they still come to the Raffles? Because it is the genuine article. They want to see the Long Bar, and imagine where the tiger was shot. They want to picture themselves shooting the damned tiger, slapping each other on the back, saying 'jolly good, old chap,' and downing their 'stengahs'. Never mind that the modern world is only a stone's throw away at the Westin. The women imagine themselves elegantly gowned, like Marlene Dietrich, champagne glass in hand, and drawing smoke through a long cigarette holder.

"It was the life — but for a very small group of people. Mainly, the colonials experienced this life only by virtue of their posting to this part of the world. Otherwise, most probably they would have led humdrum lives in some drizzly, gritty London suburb.

"The East has its mystique, and the Raffles played a pivotal part in presenting this allure. Whatever I said just now, it was then a little bit of civilization in an uncivilized world. I think that was what Maugham meant in that quotation. I dare say what I've told you so far wouldn't have evoked quite the same feelings if it had happened at a guesthouse or an ordinary hotel."

Then my grandmother breathes heavily and says, "Now enough of talking, I'll get you the dress."

She hobbles across to her wardrobe and takes out a package of gossamer tissue and hands it to me. I unwrap it and there is the dress I have seen my grandmother in, in photographs. It smells of mothballs and faintly of Mitsouko, cigarette smoke and sweat.

"I haven't had it laundered since that night," she says.

I am holding a piece of history, the real stuff. I look at my watch, it is nearly one o'clock. My grandmother has gone back to her divan. Her eyes are closed, almost as if the recall of old faces and painful events has been too strenuous. I leave quietly. I know that when I wear this outfit, I'll be wearing more than a dress, I'll be wearing the story of a life.

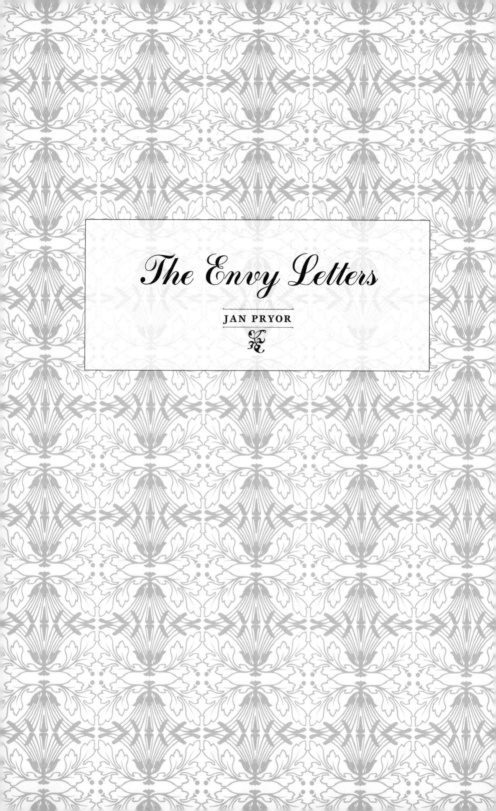

The Envy Letters

JAN PRYOR

LAST time I was here, paint flaked from these Palm Court walls like skin from a sunburned child. The building was tired and its sagging foundations groaned in sympathy with my old, aching bones.

But perhaps not so tired. The fables which surround this place, weaving myth and reality through the passage of time, will last long after the building rots into the landscape. She has been restored now but still it gives me strength to sit here, tracing the patterns of the new plaster with my slowly dimming eyes. As sun and history warm me, reaching those long-hidden places inside, I hear her old voice whispering to me through her new face, whispering through the years…

The first time, my toes showed like little pink pearls as I dug my feet into the grainy sand. Dad's big, hairy hand was clammy as it grasped mine to prevent a sudden escape and possible drowning in the water nearby. My eyes were dazzled by a tall white building across the road, taller even than the giants in my favourite bedtime book. It loomed above me like a big cake, shimmering in the baking heat, the centre of my vision and my little life.

We stayed at the cake-hotel for weeks at a time, Daddy, Mother and I. My friends were the coolies and cooks — three feet taller than me and smelling like exotic plants. How often my neck hurt from craning up to see their shiny faces and the black eyes which disappeared into creases when they smiled. My best friend had a long rope-like pigtail which nearly touched the ground, and entertained me for hours as I waited for it to be shut in a door or pulled by a child naughtier than I.

Once, my friend gave me a pair of chopsticks, which I used for digging little holes in the garden, where the banana tree went schick-schick-schick against the wall at night. Another time I used the chopsticks to make splints for my doll, which in my oddly caring way I dropped from the sweeping staircase so that I could heal its imaginary broken leg.

Sometimes I pretended to be a mouse, scurrying my way along unknown corridors, crouching down into a little ball when the big men with their shouty laughs rumbled toward me. Later, when they were sitting on the verandah, I would visit them for stories and a pat on the cheek. At night I heard them carousing, and imagined droplets of beer clinging to their whiskers as they danced and sang and slapped each other on the back.

The small dramas of my childhood were played out against a backdrop of wide passages, sloping floors and high ceilings. I even learned to count using the pendulous great lamps which hung from the beams at neat intervals. I was fascinated, too, by the patterns of light and dark cast by the latticed windows. My father, forgetting my tender years, used their silent path to explain the movement of the planets, and wished for an elder son.

Every day Daddy would take me to the beach, while my mother rested in the heat of the afternoon. Soon my cotton frock would stick to my tummy and chest, so my middle looked like a small upturned wok. I carried a perky red beach-bucket, waving it about as a symbol of proprietorship, and watched fascinated as my father's face turned a matching red, roasting inside his stuffy western clothes in the endless heat.

Even in those distant days, Raffles Hotel was famous throughout the world. My mother's long letters home would be rewarded with picture postcards from friends and sisters, all spelling out their envy at her

I carried a perky red beach-bucket, waving it about as a symbol of proprietorship…

good fortune. "How wonderful," one wrote, "to lie back with a cool drink and savour life in so famous a place."

Mother's letters were full of diamonds, which darted blue into the eyes as they reflected light from the ballroom chandeliers, and of perfume which tantalised the gentlemen as it wafted across the dining room at night. But when out-of-sorts, she pursed her lips and noted the loud behaviour of fellows in the Long Bar and wrote of bawdy performances by visiting actors. "They laugh more boisterously than anyone else," she complained. "And always so unnecessarily."

The Envy Letters, as Mother called the postcards, were one of my great joys. I thumbed the pictures constantly and imagined myself holding court in the far-off places whence they came. For several days I cherished one card down the front of my dress. It featured a plump, pink lady with small pointed teeth and read "Greetings from Birmingham". The lady was perfection in my eyes, and that grimy northern city promised more romance than I could imagine.

How unsurprising that as I grew older and wiser the tropical mystery of the East and the fabled portals of Raffles should become my ideals of romance.

The day inevitably came when my family left Singapore and the Envy Letters reached us no more. But the memory of those balmy Raffles days was only a moment away, carefully packed with my mother's original notes between sheets of tissue paper in a battered leather suitcase under my bed.

Immersed in the postcards and letters from those happy times, I needed only to close my eyes to feel the sand between my toes and the lazy fans stirring a gentle breeze across my face. Ah, Raffles, soul of my soul.

Over the years I came many times to the grand old hotel, drawn by my memories and the endorsement of others more famous than me. In turn I wrote my own Envy Letters, to children and grandchildren, sharing the joy and romance of so many long years. For them, too, Raffles became a magic place, glowing on the infinite map of travel and time.

On every visit I noted the changes, as age slowly etches the face of an old friend, and basked in the warmth of familiarity. As I wandered through the passages of my childhood and caressed the banisters, worn to a satin finish by decades of trailing hands and polishing cloths, I felt at peace yet a little sad at the passing of the years.

My childhood friend with the pigtail is no more. I remember one trip, when I found him dozing in the sun, his face brown and whiskered like an old yam, his head sunk into his bowed shoulders with the weight of age. I am no longer young myself, and think of him with sympathy down the years.

The sea is far away now, pushed from its original cradle by the relentless needs of progress. The hotel's paint no longer peels; under the bright new finish I feel the grand old lady still remains. Her whispers are quieter. The old ones are gone but the legend lives on.

There, beneath the banana leaves, a small child plays in the dirt.

The Singapore Fling

JOHN KHONG

"HAPPY Birthday, Mummy," echoed May Lin and May Ying excitedly. Su Lin beamed with joy as she blew out the candles on the cake with a tremendous puff.

"I've got to run, children or I'll be late for my tour," Su Lin added, glancing at her watch. She hastily sliced a small piece of the chocolate cake.

"Thank you, family," she cried. Su Lin quickly kissed her children and Boon Seng in succession. "We'll celebrate tonight, I promise."

Pushing the cake into her mouth, she opened the door of her white Suzuki. Soon she was driving towards her tour office. Su Lin smiled while waiting for the traffic lights to change. She considered herself the most contented if not the luckiest woman alive. At thirty-eight, she was the owner of a fairly successful tour agency. She had two adorable girls in kindergarten, a devoted husband, a cosy little executive maisonette at Bedok, and a car.

Today was special. It was her birthday — and the start of her new local tour programme which would culminate in a visit to Raffles Hotel. Raffles Hotel — the place and name meant something special to her. What it was she could not explain, but the feeling was there.

As Su Lin walked into the office, she saw Joan and Margaret whispering at the watering hole, the office pet name for the drinking fountain. Margaret grinned and beckoned Su Lin towards her. "I saw David again during lunch-time. Oh, he's so gentle and warm," purred Margaret.

Su Lin lowered her head and stared at Margaret from the corner of her glasses. "You're getting yourself into trouble when Mun Seng finds out," she lectured.

Margaret had been married to Mun Seng for five years but was still without a child. Their marriage had been on a plateau until the chance meeting of Margaret and David a month ago.

"But, Sue," protested Margaret, "he's like Prince Charming, bringing a new splendour of colour to my life."

"Fables. These are nothing but story-book fables. They do not happen in this concrete jungle," Su Lin added. She grabbed her files and hastily left the office to lead her maiden morning tour.

"Funny," she thought, "I just read about fables in the tourist guidebook to Raffles Hotel. Wasn't it the celebrated writer, Somerset Maugham, who said 'Raffles stands for all the fables of the exotic East'?"

"What hogwash," mused Su Lin to herself as the tour bus, filled with tourists, approached Raffles Hotel on Beach Road. The East was no longer exotic. Its romantic aura had been polluted by the incessant onslaught of modern western philosophies and temporal values. The stark truth was the need to work hard and eke out a living as comfortably as possible. Romances and fables were for the faint hearted idealist.

The excited crowd jostled down the bus and moved into the shelter of the spacious hotel porch in front of the lobby. Su Lin followed. As she entered the historic white building, a strange feeling overcame her. The people momentarily dimmed out of her sight. It was as if she were suspended in time, and a greater force took hold of her consciousness. The sensation melted away as fast as it had seized her. Su Lin could feel the humid heat once again. "Ladies and Gentlemen," she raised her voice quickly, "welcome to the famous Raffles Hotel."

The tour went well. The American tourists asked the most questions. It would be a usual group except that she noticed a young Caucasian man among the older travellers. He was well-built, good-looking and strangely attentive. When Su Lin spoke to the group it was as if he were not listening to her. The young man was *looking* at her, intently as if studying a piece of artwork.

The tour ended at the Long Bar where the guests were given the opportunity to sample that indigenous cocktail, the Singapore Sling. "The extensive renovation somehow has not taken away the spirit of Raffles," thought Su Lin as she took a short break at the corner of the bar. A yellow rose had fallen from the vase on the coffee table. Su Lin picked it up and her fingers played with it aimlessly.

"My... my name is Jean," a soft voice quivered, "Jean Magnan." But it sounded like 'John'.

Su Lin looked up and saw the young handsome tourist standing next to her. "Oh," replied Su Lin spontaneously, "I'm Su Lin, but just call me Sue. Everyone calls me that. Tell me, are you enjoying the tour?"

"Yes... oui... yes, of course," Jean stammered. "I'm an architecture student on attachment to the National University... University of Singapore."

Su Lin could feel the boy trembling. Under the light of the table lamp, she saw he could not be more than twenty-five. He had attractive blue eyes and a boyish

A yellow rose had fallen from the vase
on the coffee table.

face. Su Lin glanced across the room. On seeing that most of the tourists had left, she quickly stood up and apologised. "I'm sorry, Jean. We've got to move on." Su Lin did not take any notice of him for the rest of the tour. When she returned to the office, Joan was the first to greet her.

"How did the Raffles tour go?"

"Pretty good," replied Su Lin.

"Magnificent!" muttered Margaret dreamily.

"It's not all that good," corrected Su Lin.

"Whose talking about your tour?" sighed Margaret. "I'm describing my… my… dreamboat." Everyone had a good laugh.

Su Lin left the subsequent Raffles tour to Joan. She had other pressing matters to attend to. The following week, Joan burst into the office after conducting her third tour to the hotel.

"The place is spooked!" Joan exclaimed.

Su Lin looked up at her from her oval desk. "Raffles Hotel?" she asked.

"Hmm…" muttered Joan as she chewed a cookie.

"Funny, I had that strange feeling when I stepped into the hotel during the maiden tour."

"I don't mean that," interrupted Joan. "It's that young Caucasian. This is the third time I saw him at the hotel with a bunch of yellow roses. He seems to be waiting for someone. I wish I was the lucky girl!"

Su Lin dropped her pen in astonishment. "He had yellow roses on all three occasions?"

"Yes. He must be cranky or madly in love!" exclaimed Joan.

Su Lin did not answer. She soon forgot about the incident as she plunged into her mountain of paperwork.

It was Friday and she had to work late. She reached for the telephone and called home. It was eight o'clock in the evening. Boon Seng was not back yet. Probably he had to work late too. As everyone in the office had left, Su Lin thought it best to lock the office entrance for security. As she approached the door, she saw someone standing outside. "May I help you?" asked Su Lin in her usual service-oriented style. Imagine her surprise when she was greeted by a bouquet of yellow roses as the person turned round. It was the Frenchman.

"What are you doing here?" Su Lin asked.

"Sue, I just came to give you some flowers. I noticed, the other day, you liked yellow roses," Jean replied confidently.

"Oh! Not that. I was just playing with a fallen flower. Anyway, come in and take a seat," offered Su Lin.

"Sue, I have never seen a women as beautiful as you are. I've not stopped thinking about you since I saw you. Can I have dinner with you?" asked Jean point-blank.

Su Lin could not believe her ears. She had just passed thirty-eight. The last time a man said she was beautiful was so long ago that she could not remember it. Boon Seng had never called her beautiful: neat, well-dressed, a good match, yes; but not beautiful — nor had he praised her with such sincerity.

"I am sorry, Jean. I have a lot of work to do. Maybe some other time," she replied.

Jean handed the roses to Su Lin and clasped her hands tenderly. He looked up hesitantly with forlorn eyes and whispered, "Please..."

"Are Rafflesian fables about to relive themselves?" Su Lin asked herself. "Has the cosmic order run rampant?"

Against all reason and logic, Su Lin consented. "Where do you want to eat?"

"Tiffin Room at Raffles Hotel," Jean replied — looking away. The same strange sensation overwhelmed Su Lin at the mention of Raffles Hotel.

"Perhaps it should be Fables Hotel," she chuckled to herself.

"Do you mind if we ride my Harley Davidson?" asked Jean sheepishly as they walked to the car park.

"What?" demanded Su Lin. "A woman at my age?

Surely you are not serious!"

Jean was dead serious. He held her gently by the hand and led her to the larger-than-she-expected black motor cycle, glistening in the street lights. Su Lin wore her helmet clumsily. "This isn't true," she assured herself.

Luckily she had kept her hair short, she thought. Soon they were roaring down the street. She was uncomfortable with her hands, and held on to the seat cushion below her. She was self-conscious at first when they stopped at traffic junctions. She could swear that all the passengers in double-decker buses were peering down at her. The pedestrians crossing at traffic lights seemed curious too. As the bike sped, she felt the strength of the cool evening breeze brushing against her cheeks. When Joseph Conrad said of Raffles that it was 'as airy as a birdcage,' he obviously had not experienced a night ride on a motor bike!

As they ate the fragrant, spicy curry in the Tiffin Room, Jean apologised repeatedly and wiped the perspiration off his forehead. He did not eat much actually. He was too absorbed in his fascination with Su Lin. Whenever he realised that his stare was becoming obtrusive, he smiled and cast his eyes down to the food. Jean quickly regained his confidence. Su Lin found him to be delightful and charming for a man of his age. He was well-read and had a passion for life. Su Lin learned that he had been in Singapore for three months. He was working for his doctoral thesis in oriental architecture. His ancestors, he said, could be traced to French royalty, although he did not care much about it. Jean's father ran a large family enterprise in southern France, and had been continually trying without success to get Jean to help him manage the growing business.

"And what do you do when you are not studying or dating older women?" teased Su Lin.

"But you are not old," he protested quickly. "Maybe you have a few more years than me but it's the heart. You have a young vibrant heart that seeks freedom and fulfilment. I know."

"What do you for recreation?" rephrased Su Lin.

"I climb mountains," he replied. "The view from a mountain top is beyond description. Why don't you come with me one day? It will be the enchantment of my life to share a breathtaking panoramic view with you."

Su Lin smiled. It had been quite some time since she saw someone with so much zest for life.

"It's fantastic up there, I tell you," repeated Jean. "It's like having all your dreams come true, like being in paradise, like…"

"Like an exotic fable?" interrupted Su Lin.

"Yes. Yes. A wonderful unforgettable fable," replied Jean.

It was getting late. Su Lin soon found herself driving home. As she entered her flat, she saw her husband at work in the living room.

"I'm back, darling," Su Lin said, breaking the stillness of the night.

"Had your dinner, Sue?" asked Boon Seng, without looking up.

"Yes," replied Su Lin as she climbed upstairs. The children were asleep. In the shower, she felt the soothing warm water pouring all over her tired body. As she covered her face with her hands to ward off the gushing water, she could visualise Jean looking at her across the table in the Tiffin Room. She moved to the mirror and wiped away the mist on it. Staring at her reflection, she asked herself, "Am I still attractive? Smart, yes, efficient, probably; but beautiful?"

After the shower, Su Lin tucked herself comfortably in bed. "Are you coming to bed, Boon Seng?" she asked loudly.

A faint voice responded from the stairway, "No dear, I've got to finish this."

Su Lin closed her eyes and smiled. It was the most extraordinary day in her life. It was as if she had walked into a story-book of fables.

The days that followed were hectic, neutralising any remaining stardust of that evening's magic. The telephones were ringing furiously in the office. Exasperated, Su Lin picked up the next call mechanically and intoned, "Fantasy Tours, can I help you?"

"Sue, it's Jean. I missed you."

Su Lin took a deep breath and acted nonchalant. "What is it Jean? I'm quite busy now."

"Can I see you again?" he asked.

Su Lin stared out of the office glass window. "No," she muttered. "You had better spend more time on your studies. Goodbye."

She hung up, her hand trembling, still holding onto the receiver. The further ringing of the phone startled her. "Sue, please," Jean pleaded, "I beg you. I'll see you outside Har Par Villa at one o'clock today. I'll not leave until you come. Goodbye."

Su Lin was stunned. Jean was coming on pretty hard. "What's happening? This can't be true? I'm a happily-married middle-aged mother of two!"

That afternoon, Su Lin saw Jean with sun glasses on, waiting for her patiently at the entrance of the famous Tiger Balm Gardens. He greeted her with a radiant smile, waving two tickets in the air. Su Lin took out her sunglasses too and put them on.

"How did you know I'll come?" laughed Su Lin.

"Because you are a humanitarian. You save lives," he replied.

"Humanitarian?" quizzed Su Lin.

"Oh! What I meant is that if you did not turn up, I would die a slow painful death from a broken heart. You remember what happened to the Beast when Beauty did not show up?"

"More fables," remarked Su Lin, "and I'm no beauty."

"Oh yes you are. You're the most beautiful," insisted Jean. "After all we are now in the park of Chinese fables and myths!" Su Lin had never had so much fun as during the two hours they spent in the amusement park. Jean volunteered unhesitatingly for the Chinese story-telling sketch at the Four Seasons Theatre. He practically dragged the reluctant Su Lin into it. They screamed their hearts out as they rode the water sledge in the Wrath of the Water Gods Flume Ride. She squeezed Jean's hand so tight that she thought she had broken his fingers.

But Su Lin had a sobering moment when they sailed through the Chinese Purgatory in the Tales of China Boat Ride. As the grotesque figurines depicting the punishments for infidelity stared at her, she shuddered momentarily. Images of Boon Seng, the girls and Jean flashed through her mind. "These may be Chinese mythology and folklore but it is hard to dispel the beliefs," thought Su Lin. "Do Somerset Maugham's fables of the exotic East include all these contradictions?"

The week sailed by rapidly. By now Su Lin was actually looking forward to these weekly escapades with Jean. She remembered hearing Margaret once describing such planned encounters as 'luncheon affairs'. "But this is different," Su Lin reassured herself, "Jean and I are just friends — or, if it must be, good friends."

Late one afternoon, Jean called Su Lin at the office. "My dear Sue," Jean said excitedly, "let's go and fly a kite. I'll meet you at Marina Bay in half an hour."

Jean hung up. Su Lin could not believe her ears. She had never flown a kite before. She looked at her desk. Most of her schedules were completed. She might as well go.

The wind was blowing strongly in the field where Jean stood. He was holding two colourful kites. He walked towards Su Lin and gave her a kite with a spool of string.

"But how do you fly it?" asked Su Lin.

"Don't worry. The wind will do the work. Just let yourself go and things will turn out beautifully," Jean answered with a wink. True enough, in a short while Jean had his kite up. The kite was soon looking smaller as it ascended towards the clear blue sky dotted with patches of fluffy cloud.

"Here, hold the string," said Jean while he attempted to launch the other kite. Su Lin could feel the firm pull of the string as her kite soared in the sky. She saw Jean's kite rising quickly to join hers. Su Lin felt a satisfying sense of control. The kite was steady and predictable. The other kite was different. It tended to turn and spin. With adept manoeuvring, Jean brought his kite near hers.

"Take this string too," said Jean cheekily as he placed the other string quickly on Su Lin's other hand.

"No... no... Jean... don't," she shouted, "I cannot handle both."

"Yes, you can, of course," laughed Jean.

The second kite began to take a dive and tailspin. Su Lin's kite remained steady and rose even higher. She was desperate. She could not pay equal attention to both kites. She hastily moved forward to relieve the tumbling kite. In her excitement the strings of both kites become entangled. She tugged against the resistance. Jean's kite plunged into a distant tree. The string of her kite broke and set it sailing free. Without hesitation, Su Lin ran after the trailing string, followed by Jean. In the hurry, she tripped and fell into the thick grass. Jean rushed to her and knelt close, holding her soft pulsating body.

“Are you hurt, Su Lin? I’m sorry to cause this,” said Jean regretfully. Su Lin did not move. Jean became worried. He placed both his hands on her flushed cheeks.

“Su Lin, Su Lin, are you all right?” Jean asked with deep concern. Su Lin peeled open one eye and laughed. “Yes, the useless kite-flyer is well.”

Jean’s eyes met Su Lin’s. They looked at each other intensely for a moment. Then Jean reached out and gently kissed Su Lin. Su Lin closed her eyes and placed her arms around Jean pulling him on to the grass. They hugged one another tightly as their wet lips met. For that moment, time stood still for Su Lin. It was as if, like the break-away kite, she had floated into eternity.

That night during dinner at home, she looked at Boon Seng over the table. He was talking as usual, with food in his mouth, of his problems at work. Su Lin was hearing but not listening.

“If only we have staff with good attitudes today,” complained Boon Seng.

“Jean never asked if I was married. Is he taking me for a ride?” said Su Lin to herself.

“I had to fire my technician yesterday for negligence,” added Boon Seng, agitated.

“Oh my goodness. I think I have fallen in love with this boy,” Su Lin’s thought continued.

“We had to pay him a handsome packet, of course, to

appease the union," continued Boon Seng. He rattled on, while Su Lin's thoughts of Jean went deeper.

That night as she retired to bed with Boon Seng, she reached over and put her hand on Boon Seng's arm. "Darling," Su Lin asked, "do you love me?"

Boon Seng put his book down and looked at Su Lin. "What kind of question is that, Sue? Of course I do. You know I do," he added and continued reading his book.

Su Lin looked at the ceiling fan circulating above her. "Can a woman love two men at the same time?" she asked herself. She recalled the afternoon's kite-flying experience. Could she learn to handle two kites simultaneously? Would she fall and hurt herself?

On Wednesday, Su Lin was in the office by eight in the morning. She had a long day ahead. Tiger, her cat, was not eating again and she had to take her to the vet. They had had the aged feline for almost ten years. She was considered by all a full-fledged family member.

The silence of the room was broken by the ringing telephone. Su Lin was delighted. It must be Jean as he called every Wednesday. This time, he was early.

"Sue," Jean said, "can we have lunch earlier, at eleven-thirty today?"

"It's all right, but why?" asked Sue, curious.

"Nothing… nothing… at all," stammered Jean. "I'll

see you at Raffles Grill at the Raffles Hotel."

Su Lin put the phone down. "Raffles Hotel," she muttered excitedly to herself. "That Great Old Dame Of Fables and Dreams. What flight of fantasy will it transport me to this time?"

When she entered the restaurant, Jean stood up to help Su Lin into her seat.

"You didn't have breakfast today, did you?" said Su Lin playfully.

Jean forced a smile and looked down. "You look more beautiful with every passing day."

Su Lin noticed that Jean was not eating. He was acting in a strange, nervous way.

"Are you well, Jean?" Su Lin asked earnestly.

"Yes... yes," he stuttered. "I'm fine. It's just... I'm not very hungry somehow."

Su Lin did not take further notice of his behaviour until they were ready to leave.

"Su Lin," Jean whispered, looking left and right very quickly, "can we go... go upstairs?"

"Upstairs?" Su Lin repeated in surprise. "You want to shop for something?" Su Lin stared at Jean.

Jean blushed profusely. He cast his eyes down and reached into his right trouser-pocket. Clumsily, he pulled his clenched fist out and opened it on the table. Su Lin looked and saw a hotel room-key.

"I... I've booked a room so that we can be together for a while," Jean explained trembling.

"You mean..." began Su Lin.

"Yes... but only if you wish. Please think about it," he pleaded — as if innocently.

She stared at the key. A thousand thoughts raced through her mind.

"Su Lin. Don't get me wrong. Believe me, I've never slept with a woman before. I promised myself I will express my love only for the woman I truly love and adore. You are that woman."

Her mind was stabbed by a thousand needles. She liked Jean a lot, but this... this. She had never been unfaithful before. And could it be happening to her now? It must be an enacted fable, a dream turned dramatic. She gazed at the beautifully engraved room number, 44.

"In Cantonese, it's Sei-Sei or die, die," reflected Su Lin. "If I accept, it could be marital death; and if I don't, it might mean an emotional death."

Still looking at the key, Su Lin took a deep breath and uttered the irreversible words, "Jean, you go up first."

Su Lin's heart was pumping furiously as she reached Room 44. Her trembling hand reached out uncontrollably for the brass door knob. As she pushed the door open, she saw Jean sitting on the edge of the luxurious bed without his shirt on. He had a firm beautifully-contoured body covered by wavy blonde hair on the upper chest. The door slammed behind her. Jean moved quickly towards Su Lin and put his strong arms around her shaking body. She felt the warmth of Jean's smooth body radiating close to her. Their hungry lips met spontaneously. As they kissed passionately, Jean slid his right hand in between the buttons of her blouse.

Later, Su Lin lay on the bed, wrapped under the sheet, staring contentedly at her pile of clothes on the floor. The words of James Michener flashed through her mind, 'To have been young and had a room at Raffles was probably life at its best.'

Su Lin knew she was not young but she felt young. Rudyard Kipling had described Raffles Hotel as 'a place where the food is as excellent as the rooms are bad.' "How contradictory!" mused Su Lin. "And how different it is when you experience real passion again."

Su Lin saw Jean pick up her clothes and bring them to her. He brushed her hair gently away from her face and kissed her gently on the forehead. Jean sat next to her, patiently helping her to dress.

"Did I make you happy?" asked Jean earnestly.

Su Lin did not answer. It was Jean's first encounter. He was awkward and uncertain at times but his vigour and passion more than made up for his inexperience. It had been an unplanned excitement but an extremely electrifying one. It was something she had not experienced for a long time with Boon Seng. She shuddered when she thought of Boon Seng. Images began to float across her mind. This time they were the grotesque figurines at Haw Par Villa.

"Sue, did you feel nice?" asked Jean softly again. Su Lin threw her arms helplessly around Jean and held him tightly. Tears of confusion fell down her cheeks. She did not know what to say.

In the evening, when Su Lin arrived home, May Ying and May Lin rushed to hug her. "Mummy," shouted May Ying gleefully, "what did you do at work today?"

Su Lin was startled. She hesitated and quickly replied, "I had to entertain a client."

"What's 'entertain', Mummy?" asked May Lin. Su Lin stooped down and put one arm around each of her daughters. "It means to make a person happy… I mean feel nice… er… as part of business."

"Does 'client' mean someone who is also kind to you?" asked a beaming May Ying.

Before Su Lin could reply, Boon Seng joined in.

"You are all wrong," he shouted from the living room. "To entertain can mean a naughty thing also," Boon Seng chuckled loudly.

His prolonged laughter stabbed like a sharp sword through Su Lin's fragile heart. She quickly retreated to her room, disturbed and filled with deep thoughts.

Boon Seng was on leave that day. When they retired to bed that evening, he undressed Su Lin. Su Lin closed her eyes. Jean's smiling face suddenly appeared before her. Startled, she quickly opened her eyes only to see the darkness in the room.

Soon Boon Seng rolled away. It was over sooner than she expected.

"Jean is so different... so very different," Su Lin sighed, as she drifted into sleep.

It was already three in the afternoon the following Wednesday and Jean still had not called. "This is very unlike him," thought Su Lin. Wild thoughts began to fill her mind.

"Was this affair just another fling?" Su Lin feared. "'Caucasian boy entices foolish Oriental girl, Oriental girl succumbs. Caucasian boy seduces Oriental girl and leaves after the fun.'"

By six o'clock, there was still no call. Su Lin telephoned the house where Jean was a tenant. There was no reply. Su Lin's fear turned quickly to anger. "Have I been taken for a ride?" she asked. "Am I like a grown-up Gretel lured into the fabled woods to see my chocolate house of dreams turned into a horrid witch's abode?"

That night, Su Lin skipped dinner, pretending that her gastric pains had returned. She hated Jean for his sweet words and charm. She turned and tossed the whole night in bed. Luckily, Boon Seng was a heavy sleeper.

The next day dragged on. Jean did not call. Su Lin's ego was completely devastated. She prided herself on being an excellent judge of character. Yet deep down she knew it was not only her self-esteem that was bruised. She felt for Jean. She had, for some unexplainable reason, fallen in love with him. She had let herself become a lover of two men.

Her heart was not in her work. She left the office early, resigned to the miserable thought that she was probably the object of an indiscreet sexual liaison: a Singapore fling.

On Friday, Su Lin had to lead the Raffles Hotel tour, as Joan was taken ill. Su Lin felt too despondent to do anything well. On top of her emotional turmoil, Tiger had taken a turn for worse the night before. But business was business. She braced herself, and was relieved when the tour ended once again at the Long Bar. "Ladies and Gentleman," explained Su Lin almost monotonously, "this is where you can enjoy the famous Singapore Fling."

Hilarious laughter echoed throughout in the room. Su Lin looked puzzled for a moment before she regained her presence of mind.

"I'm sorry," she forced a smile, "what I meant was the Singapore Sling."

More laughter broke out.

"What the heck?" thought Su Lin. "What's the difference: sling or fling. I've drunk the bitter cup of the Singapore Sling."

She looked slowly round the walls of the room. "Raffles Hotel — the origin of fables," she muttered. "Yes, but it's here too, where dreams are shattered." That warm romantic feeling that she felt every time she was in the hotel had now turned to a prolonged biting chill.

When Su Lin arrived home, she was greeted by the loud sobbing of her daughters. "Tiger's dead," cried May Lin bitterly.

"She just fell asleep," said May Ying, wet with tears.

Sorrow was now Su Lin's speciality. She held both girls, each by one hand, and tried to comfort them. "It's all right. Tiger was a good cat. She's happy in heaven now."

Su Lin knew she would miss the familiar lovable cat but, to her, a cat was a cat. It was perhaps better for her to go than to suffer in pain.

Boon Seng was a little late that evening. Su Lin and

her daughters waited at the dining table for him to return. Soon the door opened. Boon Seng was waving his newspapers excitedly as he walked into the room.

"There's a dead hero born every day!" he remarked with a smile. Su Lin's mind was elsewhere.

"Here's a report of a brave mountaineer who gave his life for his friend in Nepal," Boon Seng continued, as he sat down. "He actually descended into a deep crevice to haul out a fallen climber."

The word 'mountaineer' cut through Su Lin's heart like a sharp razor. She froze in silence. From where she sat, she could see a photograph of a frightfully familiar young face. "Luckily, he's not a Singaporean," Boon Seng rattled on, as he stabbed his fork into the chicken. "Let me see… his name is…"

Su Lin's face turned pale. She held her breath as she felt a sudden coldness seizing her body.

"His name is Jean… Jean… Mag… Magnan."

Two large teardrops rolled down Su Lin's cheeks. She quickly wiped them away with her hand but to no avail. More tears poured down her face. Next, she was sobbing loudly with her wet face buried in her hands. Su Lin quickly stood up and ran upstairs to her bed. She was soon crying and trembling wildly. "It wasn't a fling. I should have known him better," cried Su Lin to herself. "He truly loved me. How could I betray his trust and cast doubt on my honourable dead hero!"

Boon Seng, puzzled by the outburst, quickly chased after her, followed by the children. He put his hand on Su Lin's shoulder and asked her gently, "What's wrong, darling?"

Su Lin did not answer. She could not hide it anymore. The truth must finally be revealed but she did not care, at least not any more. She would face the consequences bravely. She lifted her head to speak.

"Daddy," interrupted May Ying suddenly. "It's Tiger. Mummy is upset over her death."

Su Lin was stunned. She gaped at May Ying, with residual tears still rolling off her cheeks.

"Darling," consoled Boon Seng, "it's only a cat. We'll get another cat. I promise you."

Su Lin's mind wandered wildly.

"Jean my dearest," thought Su Lin, "please forgive me. I'm going to miss you terribly." That night was the longest night in her life.

Throughout the following week, Su Lin felt an emptiness within her. Joan had a stubborn flu. Su Lin dreaded taking the Raffles Hotel tour again. As she entered the magnificent edifice, she felt a coldness within her. The exotic palace had become a mausoleum. She could feel the presence of Jean in every step she took. Vivid scenes glided through her mind: Jean listening attentively to her tour, the dinner at the Tiffin Room, the hotel room where she felt him within her.

Su Lin wiped away an occasional tear from the corner of her eyes as time went along. A week dragged by. She thought she felt better until she saw an unusual letter addressed to her in the office. The yellowish envelope bore a colourful Nepalese stamp. Su Lin glanced at the familiar handwriting. It was from Jean! With trembling hands, she ripped open the envelope. Clumsily, she pulled out the note and read it.

"Darling," wrote Jean in his excellent hand, "I am about to climb the peak this morning and I somehow feel compelled to write to you by some strange force. I do know you are married, and happily too, with two beautiful daughters. You must have wondered why I have never asked you about this. Love makes no presuppositions. True love is a heavenly rarity. It strikes suddenly and demands immediate unfettered responses. I love you as you are. The bars of conventions cannot restrain me from you. I shall return soon and love you even more. And even if I don't, we'll become stronger, with our passionate relationship adding a richer dimension to our lives. True love can only bring joy."

Su Lin looked out of the window into the busy street, unable to control her emotions. She pressed the letter gently to her breasts.

"I love you much more than you will ever know," Jean had signed off.

She closed her eyes and whispered helplessly, "Jean, I love you with all my heart too."

Six months passed swiftly. Jean's belated note brought the much needed comfort Su Lin needed. She must believe Jean's conviction that true love could only bring joy, not pain or remorse. Time, too, played its part in healing her heart.

Boon Seng pulled his car up outside Raffles Hotel and Su Lin and the girls scampered out. "Wow, Mummy," exclaimed May Ying, "what a lovely hotel. What a place to celebrate Mothers' Day!"

"Strange. I suddenly have a grand feeling," May Lin added.

Su Lin smiled as the wind swept aside part of her hair. She too had a feeling: not the strange awesome sensation she used to have; nor that numbing chill. It was entirely different: it was a good soothing feeling.

Boon Seng walked towards them.

"Wasn't it the celebrated Somerset Maugham who commented that 'Raffles stands for all the fables of the exotic East'?"

"Darling, you mean a place where romantic fables become a reality and dreams and fantasies are actualised?" said Su Lin.

"Something like that," replied Boon Seng with a laugh.

"That's impossible," teased Su Lin.

"Why?" asked Boon Seng.

"Because my secret fables are all fulfilled in you." Su Lin blushed, reaching out to hug her husband.

Boon Seng reciprocated. "Are you happy, dear? Very happy?"

"Yes," purred Su Lin without hesitation, clinging on to Boon Seng tightly. "True love can only bring joy."

As she looked over Boon Seng's shoulder across the courtyard of the hotel, she could have sworn she saw Jean standing there, smiling approvingly with his bouquet of yellow roses.

The Dragon Dance

KAMLA ROOPANI

THREE moustached men sat on the verandah of a hotel suite. Sunlight slanting through the leaves of a flowering tree that grew in the courtyard below and splayed its branches over the verandah, touched the balding pates of the men, deep in conversation.

Mike Edwards, whose moustache was a silver streak on a slowly-tanning face, was saying, "Phew, but the humidity does get you at times." He rubbed his brow with an ice-soaked napkin, but was reluctant to move into the artificially-lit, pastel interior of his room.

"But it never really gets too unbearable — the climate of this place is as organised as the people. There are days of relentless temperatures and then, like a sentinel in the sky, the merciful rain-general takes care of everything," said John Rivers; and, as he spoke, his moustache shot up and down with the precision of black boots in a march-past. He scanned the skies, almost expecting to see a grey pall smudge the blue skies.

"And there are other compensations, you know," said the third man, Ian Mason, who nursed, with some pride, a bushy Rajput moustache. He spoke as he eyed a dark, slender woman with a fashionable bob crossing the courtyard below.

The three companions spoke half-in-jest and half-in-earnest, unable to hide the expansive joy of being in a country as tantalising as this one. They had been recruited into the same multinational company and, until housing was provided in sleek residential apartments-for-expatriates, each had been put up at the fabled Raffles Hotel.

Their first encounter had been in the hotel's courtyard, where they sat next to each other but alone at their respective tables, and struck up a conversation.

They found themselves agreeing on a number of things. They agreed that the local food would take some getting used to. They agreed that Singapore was an interesting city; one with a mind of its own, one that was seeking to create an impact on the rest of the world, with the admirable verve of a small nation. And they agreed, although this was an unspoken agreement, that their posts here would in some way help push aside cultural frontiers; for hitherto, while each had travelled extensively, not one had settled anywhere outside his native district in England.

So here they were, temporary inheritors of their forefathers' colonial surroundings — and not without feelings of ancestral pride.

"An interesting thing happened to me the other day," continued Mason, still eyeing the dark beauty, and wondering secretly whether there would be a chance meeting later on. "You know, I was at an open-air cafe at Boat Quay, and opposite me there was this enchanting pair of eyes looking in my direction, their intent obvious. So — just out of curiosity, mind you — I strolled down to my charmer's table, and looked down at her. And what did I see, but the chest of a man… Although, the real ones have nary a hair on their skins," he concluded, with a knowing wink.

His acquaintances chortled. They were pleased with the effect of the sun on their skins, pleased with the novelty of their experiences and, in general, pleased with themselves for having earned a part in it all.

There was, however, an element of discomfort in their pleasure. The sun was causing rivulets of perspiration to run down their foreheads and backs. They clasped chilled drinks in their hands and were silent for a moment, thinking of the cooler clime they had left behind.

Suddenly, they heard an explosion of sound. Startled, all three looked up — and then down into the bougainvillaea-fringed patio where the sun played hide-and-seek between small, vivid flowers. Winding and twisting its way down the marbled corridors, past the coterie of prestigious shops, was a monstrous beast spitting smoke from flared nostrils — all bulging eyes and writhing body — then a clash of cymbals and a shout of human voices.

Edwards whistled softly. "Raffles stands for all the fables of the exotic East," he muttered, remembering a famous quotation he had read somewhere.

The other two nodded their heads, spellbound by their first encounter with the shattering Dragon Dance. Rivers was reminded, suddenly, of a movie clip he had seen at a friend's place once, of skewered tongues and multiple arms, of the religious rites of dark-skinned locals.

To be sure — this was a civilized place. Nowhere else could there be such manifestations of progress, of a thrusting economy, of a sophisticated people, of a modern exterior. But that was the problem. Supposing it was... just an exterior?

They did not know why or how, but suddenly the three men did not feel so sure of themselves, or of their new environment, any longer. The crescendo of cymbals ebbing away had left in its wake an uncomfortable sensation.

Edwards thought of a pale wife and two pale children, with their aversion to summer heat, and wondered if they would cope. Rivers' mind lingered on past associations, on the sense of detachment that leaving them had evoked, on the trail of promises to keep-in-touch he had left behind, but which he knew he would never fulfil.

And Mason asked himself if he had done the right thing, after all, in leaving behind an accommodating mistress — would there, perhaps, be an alternative source of comfort here?

Overwhelmed by the sun's relentless rays and the riotous profusion of colours and sounds, the three men retreated to their respective rooms.

She was a Lady

REBECCA BILBAO

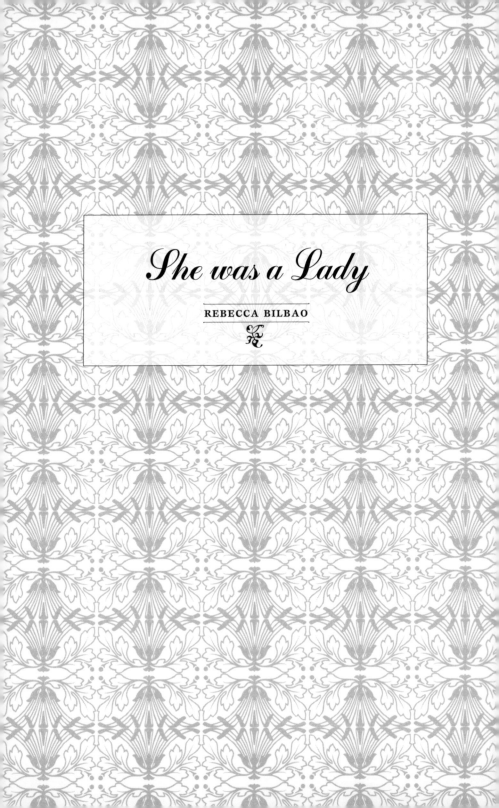

SHE was a lady. Dressed in black with pearls around her neck and at her ears, she sat day after day in the gardens and quiet verandahs of the Raffles, a startling contrast to the exotic greenery. She spoke quietly with other guests, and sewed or wrote letters home. She moved with the grace and control of a real lady.

Two gentlemen, residents of Singapore, were discussing her openly. "Her age?" challenged the first.

"She's quite young actually," replied the second gentleman, "in her early twenties, and a widow of course. Quite tragic actually, childless and seemingly still in a state of shock — a trance of quiet acceptance of her situation — totally allowing the older, wiser ladies in residence at the Raffles to look after her and make her decisions for her, as of course she should. Why, she is here now at the insistence of the Governor's wife, who would not hear of her living alone in her house on Mount Faber."

A quiet murmur that did not carry held the next question. The second gentleman replied, just as quietly.

"What happened?" He cleared his throat. "Well, the usual I suppose; she had come out from the eastern United States with her new husband and they had scarcely moved into their abode after a brief stay here, when he came down with one of the terrible fevers we have, and died. She's not destitute you know. He was quite well situated, and the company is in good hands. But she seemed in such a state of shock that the kindly Lady X insisted she move right back to the Raffles and wait, before making any decision on what to do next. I'm sure H.E.'s wife wanted to make sure that she was not in a delicate condition before embarking on such a long journey home by herself."

"And so she stayed?" asked a thirty-something man who had taken some interest in the conversation.

"Why, yes, of course she has taken the advice. She is a lady and a young one at that; she must accept the advice given to her, and now she is waiting to see what the next guidance will be." The eldest of the three was in his early sixties, and had daughters of his own.

"Have you spoken with her?" the third speaker enquired.

"Yes, on several occasions. She is actually very well read, and enjoyable to talk to without being opinionated at all," came the cool reply of the fatherly gentleman, whose own wife was known to be quite opinionated.

"Where is she going now?" All eyes turned to look at the lady in question, and followed her across the courtyard with its tall fluted central fountain that gave an illusion of coolness and masked the sounds of the city beyond.

The first gentleman paused and looked at his silver pocket-watch. The time was three o'clock, the time when ladies began to prepare for afternoon tea. He explained her destination to his companions; they watched in silence as she moved smoothly with erect carriage past them in the direction of the hotel's Tiffin Room. The youngest man was regretting that such a young and beautiful woman should be in mourning, and so unavailable for courtship, since there was a complete lack of suitable female companionship for a single man on the island of Singapore, indeed in all of Malaya.

He decided, widow or not, that he would seek out her company for some quiet conversation during the evening dinner-with-dancing, as she was sure to attend. It was customary among Singapore society to gather for Sunday evening dinner at the Raffles, attracted by the pleasure and comfort afforded by the surroundings.

She did not love him, she decided at last. She hadn't known him well enough to truly love him. Perhaps that is why she felt so peaceful about his death. She did feel sad about his particular tragedy — that there were none to miss him save herself. But she could not lay claim to any deeper emotions.

But neither did she have any plan of what to do next. She had alienated herself from her own family by marrying a Briton and moving with him to Singapore. Her family had all predicted hardship and tragedy for her, and their harsh judgment had hurt her deeply. She was not yet ready to return to her family and bear their 'I told you so' variants.

Money was not an issue she need worry about ever again. But her blank-looking future was worrying, and so she allowed herself to be comforted by the ladies of Singapore society. She took peace and comfort from quiet contemplation of her exotic surroundings and the lovely Raffles Hotel. Daily she ventured out to view the quaint, the odd and the extreme of the busy, commercial city that was Singapore, in the company of one lady or another. They would take a trishaw and poke about the merchants for silks and *objets d'art*, before the real heat of the day descended.

By the noon hour she would return to the Raffles, grateful for its stalwart presence amidst the confusion of the city. Within the grounds of this historic place she was experiencing a degree of freedom she had not known at home. There were no pre-conceptions about her that she had not herself communicated. There were no servants to manage, no brothers to look after and no harsh great-aunts to march in and criticize how she coped with the tasks and duties inherent in membership of one of New York's first families.

She supposed that she had married as much out of a wish to leave behind all her 'duties' to her family and name, as out of any love for her husband. With him gone, she was now enjoying the first real 'vacation' that a woman could expect: nothing to manage, and at no one's beck and call. There were really no plans that needed to be made besides what to wear for today's tea or who to go on an outing with tomorrow. She was truly enjoying the experience; for in her previous life she had been protected more than she liked and cosseted not at all.

For her the Raffles was a dream come true. If she wanted something, it appeared. If she wanted to be left alone with her thoughts, that too was respected. The service was excellent and the food was delightful. And, best of all, none of it was her responsibility to manage.

So she let the days slip past her, unthinkingly. The first ship home came and went, barely noticed save for the change of company. Most of the new arrivals suffered from the heat and so were only lively when dining or dancing in the relative cool of the great ballroom. In deference to the heat, the dancing was mild compared to the American way. She of course did not dance. It would have been disrespectful of her late husband to do so. And she was very respectful of his memory. But she attended the dances, watching and listening, allowing the scene to lap over her like the sound of waves.

She loved dinner for the excellence of it. One of her own torments before had been the planning of menus that pleased both her and the arbitrary tastes of her brothers. Here she delighted in the variety of dishes, those of European origin and the fiery Oriental fare. Every meal was a delightful adventure.

After dinner she joined the ladies in their corner of the room, enjoying the movement of air created by the electric fans and the sound of chattering tongues. She said little, but learned a great deal by listening to the conversation of the older lively and worldly married ladies present. The conversation never seemed to vary far from a litany of illnesses, troubles of bearing and raising children, and vagaries of servants. They one and all despaired of running a proper household in such a place; and disparaged in general the state of humanity outside the walls of the Raffles — which was seen by one and all as the bastion of good taste and necessary comfort in Singapore and Malaya.

At first all of this affected her not at all. She listened in an oddly detached mood, not really taking it in. Years later she would be able to review those scenes in her head with startling clarity. She simply sat and listened, looking at everyone and everything.

After a time, towards the beginning of her second month at the Raffles, she began to take to heart some of what she was hearing. The trials and angst of these women showed her that her own life with her brothers had not been so bad. They were not husbands to own and break her heart at will. And they would not give her children to break her body and health. In quiet reflection she decided that being in the single state had its advantages.

She also began to take in some of the male conversations that swirled around her. The concerns of international business, politics and society were all aired in knowledgeable fashion; and they quite fascinated her after a time.

She took to seating herself quietly with a bit of fancy sewing or a sheaf of paper for letter writing, near

She simply sat and listened, looking at everyone and everything.

where the men gathered during the day. And she listened as they debated the issues that troubled or irritated them. She also borrowed books from the small collection shared by guests of the hotel and read them in the privacy of her room. She learned as much as she could of the issues of the day, though she spoke no opinion aloud. The memory of her aunts' admonishments about the risks of offending anyone with the idea that she (a woman) was actually listening to the issues of the day, kept her silent.

By the end of the second month she knew what she did not want in her future. She did not wish to marry, to have children, or to keep house in Asia. But she did wish to know more about the world and to influence its doings. So, with this thought in mind, she booked her passage, not home to New York, but to Europe. There she would join the society of very busy ladies active in the cause of women's suffrage. She carried with her the memory of her months at the Raffles Hotel, and the inspiration it provided as a comfortable and quiet place, amidst exotic confusion, for reflection and rejuvenation of the soul.

A Parting Gift

JAN PRYOR

MY GRANDMOTHER was a strange old lady, full of wandering thoughts about the faraway places she visited as a young girl. Her memories clung to her like the pollen of summer flowers, and bore fruit as stories when the long New Zealand winter closed in.

Every year we kids would spend the winter holidays at Granna's beach house, cooped up by the bad weather and begging for stories to insulate ourselves from the cold outside.

"Tell us another one!" The cry was as plaintive as the call of the seagulls, which we watched wheeling on the wind.

Our grandmother kept us wrapped warmly in her memories and imaginings as we huddled by the fire in her dark, wood-panelled front room. While the sea thundered and the rain hurled itself against the windows, she would drip-feed us stories of tropical downpours, which she said sounded the same as New Zealand rain but left gently steaming paths and the scent of sweet flowers and fresh earth in their wake.

Granna's best stories were set in the corridors of Raffles, a rambling old hotel in Singapore, the island where she spent her honeymoon with our long-departed Gramp. In my limited experience, 'raffles' were competitions where you won strange prizes that Mother tucked away under the stairs. But in Granna's world, Raffles became a mysterious place which I pictured in my mind as a cross between a fairground and Wellington Railway Station — with its squat, solid columns and echoing halls. The Raffles stories were full of sparkling romance, tame monkeys, exotic people and unfamiliar events. We listened in awe to tales of long whiskers, stumpy old men and foreign personalities who set up camp in the hotel and drew their own drink-soaked portraits of the people and the times.

Granna's very best Raffles story was delivered on my seventh birthday, like a special gift she had saved for the right moment. It was about a tiger, which looked at her with gleaming eyes before it was shot at dawn, trapped under the floor of a billiard room. I had never seen such a room and longed to visit Old Grundy's pub down at the beach to see the animals I imagined hanging from lanterns and sprawled across the green-covered tables.

By bedtime, Granna's tiger was huge in my mind. I saw its shadowy body leaping in dark corners and heard its roar as she tucked me into bed in my cold attic room.

"Too much cake," Granna said with a wrinkly smile — her breath showing like a delicate puff of smoke, such as I'd seen from hunters' guns as they stalked jungle beasts in the movies.

The day after the tiger, it was still too wet to go outside. To lift our dampened spirits, Granna showed us her wedding photos. They were peopled with ladies in frothy dresses and feathered hats, all hand-coloured by a chap in Australia, where Granna and Gramp had stopped on their way home from Malaya. The turquoise rivers and pink skies painted on to the black-and-white photos only added to the mystery of the East. One picture showed Raffles Hotel, settled like one of Granna's ladies in its grounds; and not at all like the stony, cold railway station I had imagined. I looked everywhere for the tiger but I didn't even see its tail.

When the holidays ended, we went home to the city;

but Granna's exotic tales remained much in my mind. As I grew older, some of the stories faded like her wedding pictures, but others grew and became part of me, rather as vines wrap themselves irrevocably around the trunks of trees, becoming part of them. In years to come I made my own visits to the East, sailing gently through the hazy archipelago of islands and sweating through steamy jungles to distant villages, to be greeted by skinny dogs and chubby children. As I meandered through tiger country in Java and Sumatra I remembered my Granna's rainy-time stories, and smelled the flowers and earth she had brought to life.

A chance encounter brought me to Singapore where, with thumping heart, I went to meet Raffles Hotel, the 'memory' of which I had carried so long in my mind. I feared it would be changed beyond Granna's recognition; but the fabled atmosphere remained.

I stayed a few days, enjoying the faint, quirky breezes in the halls and the quiet, settled feeling of an old lady at peace with herself. When it rained I sat on damp cushions on the verandah, imagining my honeymoon grandparents, arm-in-arm on their way to tiffin. Again I heard the story of the tiger but, in grown-up fashion, I gave away the eye-witness version Granna had given me and filed the tale under 'legend' in the cardboard boxes of my mind.

When Granna died, my brother and I went to the old house by the beach to sort out her things. It was August, and bitterly cold. In the attic — no longer my childhood camp — Granna's history was piled high, blocking the light from the window, where once again the rain was beating hard to be let in.

Buried two feet under a pile of papers, I found her wedding album, carefully bound with cotton tape to an old hat box. The faded pink and silver stripes of the box reminded me of candy and days long gone. A shipping tag was pasted to the stripy side, its brittle brown paper spotted with age, like the backs of Granna's hands the last time I saw her. I could have sworn I smelled frangipani, but the fleeting scent faded as dust from the box drifted up my nose. I opened it, expecting to see a worn feathered hat — like those adorning the ladies in the wedding photos — crumpled inside like a sad, dead bird.

But no. My wonderful Granna had left one last gift. Deep inside the candy-pink box, under musty postcards and long-forgotten souvenirs of her travels in Malaya, I finally found my tiger: well, the tip of its tail, delicately clasped in a handmade silver setting. The spidery letters engraved on the clasp whispered the truth of her

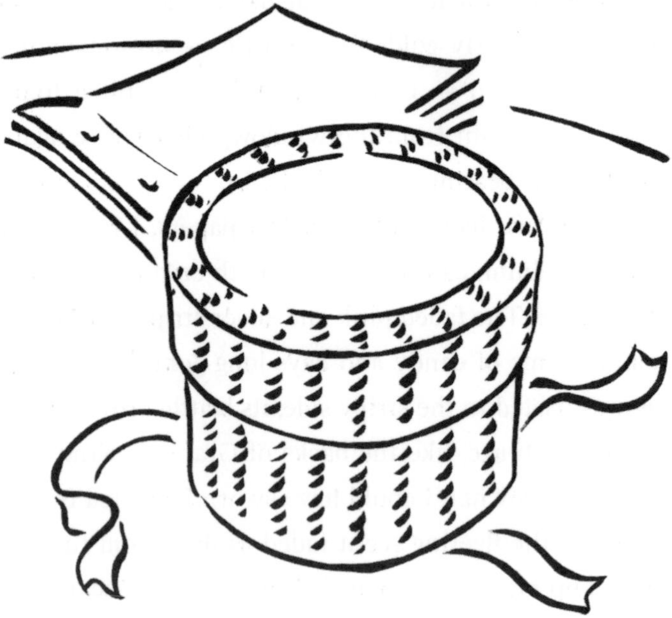

My wonderful Granna had left one last gift.

very best story: “Shot at Raffles Hotel, Singapore, August 1902.”

Beyond Reason

KHUSHWANT SINGH

IT HAD been five days since I was last at Raffles Hotel. And the events that I had undergone meanwhile were traumatic to say the least. I felt drained, as I sat on the hotel bed. There was an emptiness in my heart, and a sense of failure filled my mind. I was unable to stay in my room any more. Quickly donning my jacket, I fled downstairs. I was blind to people along the corridors. On impulse, I made for the garden.

The day was cloudy and not too warm. I had checked in at about five o'clock and it was only six now. The eternity spent in my room had only lasted an hour. Soon it would be dark and the nightmares would return.

I looked around the garden, which usually brought me much pleasure; but today I saw nothing. I did not feel complete, as if I had left a part of myself in that strange village in Pahang. What was it that I'd lost? Or was it just a feeling of loss? But that was not my character. I was Mr Rational himself. Feelings didn't affect me. To clear the aching pain, I forced myself to recollect the events that had taken place.

I was in my third year, studying herbal medicine at a Berlin university. To complete my thesis on tropical herbal remedies, I had set out for the jungles of Malaysia. A colleague was to accompany me, but he was taken ill. It didn't make sense for me to cancel my trip, so I came alone.

My family was fairly well off, so I flew first class and naturally arranged for accommodation at the Raffles Hotel. Upon arrival, I was very impressed. It resembled the glorious architecture of old German buildings. I didn't want to lose much time, so my initial stay was only for a day before I set out on my expedition.

I made my own way to Johor Baru. Across the Causeway, I hired an old Mercedes taxi — what else for a German? — to take me to Kuantan. Despite its solid appearance, it was a real boneshaker. The trip was unexciting. For most of the time we raced through acres of orderly rubber estates and palm oil plantations. The journey was punctuated by small towns. The monotony got to me and I was about to nod off, but I willed myself to stay awake. I did not trust the driver, and if I fell asleep he could drive into one of the side roads and rob me. Deep down, I realised it would be very uncharacteristic of the locals to do such a thing. He was quite a friendly sort of chap, but there was a probability that it could happen. So I stayed awake.

Instead, I studied the 'shopping list' of fauna samples I was to collect. It did cross my mind to find out a little about the country we were passing through. I could have asked the taxi driver, but then such knowledge was not necessary to my thesis. Anyway, it did not look as if I could learn anything of consequence. So, why waste my time?

I disembarked at Kuantan and hired another taxi, this time a very old Toyota. There was no other make, and it seemed to be the best maintained vehicle at the taxi depot. I showed its driver the name of the village I wanted to go to. With his fingers, he indicated that the taxi-ride would be eight dollars. What a fool, I thought. If I'd been the taxi driver, I would have charged eighty dollars. How would a foreigner with little scraps of paper know any better?

This time the ride was only two hours, before we came to a small village. My contact man was there and he had arranged for a river boat to take me further inland. Together we boarded the boat. It was then that I had my first taste of the culture of these natives. The captain was nowhere to be found, despite having been told to stand by for my arrival. Regardless of my grumbling, no one seemed to be in a hurry. The two boatmen stood on the dock smoking and talking. The man who was supposed to make the arrangements for me, instead of trying to find the captain, invited me to have a cup of coffee at the nearby coffee shop. I was in no mood for such pleasantries and refused.

Forty-five minutes later, the Chinese captain appeared; like everyone I had come across that morning he was in a good mood. His eyes were twinkling and he greeted me heartily. I replied with an ungracious nod, to express my disapproval. Taking their own sweet time, they cast off and we headed upstream.

The captain tried to strike up a conversation with me. His English was meagre, and it sounded as if he thought in another language which he then translated into English. Very much like Germans who try to speak English but whose grammar and sentence structure is completely German. However, I still bore a grudge against him for making me wait, and I was not co-operative.

The boat took three and a half hours to reach the kampung where I was to be based for two days. I hadn't expected very much but what I saw disappointed me: dwarfed by an enormous hill, it was just a scattering of huts sited behind the creaky jetty.

I climbed out of the boat onto the jetty, and my haversack and the pack containing my tent and provisions were unceremoniously dumped next to me. I was shocked. I had imagined that someone would follow me into the village to make introductions and help me settle down. Before I could say a word, the boat was on its way. The captain cheerfully wished me "Happy luck!" This was his version of "Good luck!"

The children were the first to come running, greeting me with cries of "Johnny! Johnny!" To them, every white man was 'Johnny'. Remembering my agenda, I headed directly for the biggest hut in the village. This, I deduced, belonged to the headman.

The headman had heard the boat coming, and was standing on the verandah of his hut. He was in his mid-fifties, wearing a faded sarong and a light-blue traditional shirt.

I handed him the letter of introduction that had been written for me by the Malay translator in Singapore. He read it carefully, mouthing each word, a sure indication of his literacy level. Once he had finished, he called to someone in the hut. A lad of about sixteen appeared, and the headman gave him his instructions.

The boy approached me and said in broken English that he was the one that had been hired to assist me. He told me his name was Dollah. I immediately asked him to show me round the kampung so I could find an appropriate place to pitch my tent.

The village was a small one, with seven huts of varying sizes. However there was an eighth hut, that was three-quarters destroyed by fire. The charred planks stood like some monument. Crows seemed to have made it their home, and Dollah took a wide detour so as not to pass close to it.

I had asked Dollah about this hut, but all he said was an abrupt "No talk! No talk!"

When I chose my camping site, Dollah was struck dumb. I had no intention of living in close proximity to the 'natives' and had chosen a site some twenty metres from the nearest hut and quite close to the river. Dollah found his tongue and mumbled something about a giant 'buaya'. However his buaya was of no concern to me. After he left, I looked up my Malay/English dictionary. A buaya was a crocodile. So what? I pitched my tent, ate a bar of chocolate and settled down to sleep. My last thought was of Dollah and his giant crocodile. "Superstitious little blighters," I thought.

The next day, I got Dollah to lead me up the hill behind the village. Although young, Dollah was extremely stocky; he had a scar running diagonally across his forehead. We left around eight o'clock. It was tough trekking up the hill. The incline was rather steep and I was sweating heavily after only a few minutes. Dollah hardly perspired. While I was intent above all on making haste, Dollah walked at his own pace. These people placed no value on time.

The trail led through dense jungle, and I stopped frequently to check the fauna. When the plants looked interesting, I cut off a few leaves, wrapped them up in plastic and tucked the package into my sling-bag.

By noon, we were about half-way up. Of the village we could see nothing. I signalled to Dollah and sat down beside a gushing stream. Sardonically, I asked Dollah if the giant buaya was around, knowing full well that it was a stupid question. Dollah took me seriously and replied that there were no crocodiles up here.

The morning exercise had made me very hungry. I took out my biscuits and water-bottle. I offered some to Dollah, but he shook his head. Instead he dug out a packet, that seemed to be a piece of folded leaf, and unwrapped it. Inside, was rice and some fish. He ate ravenously with his hands, while squatting on his haunches, the way I had seen the boatman sit. I had tried it but within a few minutes my legs ached terribly. Getting up from such a pose increased the agony. I had to move my legs for some time before the pain went away.

My meal over, I leaned against a tree and looked at

the river. Everything else was slow here. The heat and humidity made me sleepy. But I forced myself to stay awake. I for one believed that you can control your actions with your mind. After an hour had elapsed, I stood up. Dollah slowly got to his feet and we prepared to move again.

I pointed in the direction I wanted to go. Dollah was aghast. “Situ ada orang gila! Orang gila, tahu!” I didn’t want to waste time, so I just started walking. ‘Orang’ was man or people. But what was ‘gila’? The dictionary revealed that it meant mad. So there was a mad man around. No, the only madman in the vicinity was Dollah.

But my interest was piqued and I felt a certain force pulling me, as if I were destined to go in that direction. I walked ahead. The guide repeated his warning several times, but kept following me. I seemed to know the way. Had I been here before, in some past life? I brushed the thought away. It was utter nonsense.

We had been walking for about forty minutes when we came to a clearing. The guide stayed at the fringe of the clearing. I saw a small hut and I headed towards it. A hen scurried away clucking noisily at the intrusion.

I shouted a greeting, and a man’s head poked out of the tiny window. He didn’t seem surprised to see me.

I stopped in my tracks when he said in fluent English: "You took your time getting here."

I asked him if he were expecting me. He answered abruptly: "In a way, yes!" In what way, he did not explain; and I was too stunned to ask. He came out of the miserable hut and squatted on his haunches. I sat down on a boulder.

His English was the best I'd heard from a native. I complimented him on this, but he brushed it aside and merely said we didn't have much time. He told me that there was going to be a spate of accidents in the village and only I could prevent it. By now I was thoroughly perplexed and demanded that he tell me how he knew I was going to meet him. He didn't even acknowledge my question. Instead he repeated that there was no time left, and that I had to 'take care of' the giant crocodile.

How I was going to do that was beyond me. I had no gun. The only weapon in my possession was a Swiss army knife, and the devil himself couldn't get me to 'take care of' a crocodile with that. But before I could object, the old man said that he would provide me with a powerful 'medicine' that would make the giant crocodile go away so that its spirit could rest.

"What spirit?" I asked. I insisted on the whole story, but he shook his head. However, the look on my face must have made him change his mind, because he started to recount a bizarre tale. Mine is a shortened, tidied-up version.

Many years ago, there was a young girl who lived in the small village at the bottom of the hill. An orphan since birth, she was cared for by an old childless couple. The girl was very different from the other children. She didn't play with them. Instead, she used to disappear into the forest, and stay there for hours. Men going into the jungle claimed they saw her surrounded by wild deer, and that she could summon animals to come to her. The stories grew more fantastic with each telling, and soon the villagers grew afraid of her. They branded her a witch, and banished her from the village. The childless people who had adopted her tried to refute the accusation; but, in a fit of rage, the headman at that time ordered their hut to be burned. In a final show of defiance, the old couple stayed in their hut and were burned alive. Within a few months, accidents started to happen. The headman's wife was bitten by a snake and died in terrible agony. The headman's sampan was found overturned and his body was never discovered — a terrible fate for a Muslim. There were no eyewitnesses, but the story of a giant crocodile attacking the sampan in mid-stream gained wide credence. The villagers claimed that the little witch was behind it all.

The villagers' fishing traps were destroyed repeatedly. Even harmless wild animals turned vicious and attacked the hunters. The villagers became fearful.

I was their solution, it seemed. According to the old man, I possessed a certain force. I hardly understood the whole thing, and I did not want to get involved. I decided to leave on the pretext of going to look for Dollah, my guide.

The old man shouted at me that Dollah was not there. But I still went to look for myself. I called out to Dollah a couple of times but there was no reply. He must have rushed back to the village to tell them that I was with the madman. Untrustworthy ingrate.

So, I was truly stuck with the old man. Darkness fell swiftly and he offered me a thin mat to sleep on. I didn't have my tent, so I decided to spend the night on the verandah. It had been a long day, and I had no difficulty in falling asleep.

My sleep was disturbed by an eerie dream. It started with the frightening sensation of not being able to open my eyes. I was surrounded by fog. The anxiety of not being able to wake up and yet being awake was agonising. Then slowly my vision became clear and I was swimming with a young woman. Both of us were fully clothed. However I did not feel the water at all. I couldn't see her face, but I remember that she moved her legs very much as a crocodile moves its tail.

I felt the urge to ask her if she were the giant crocodile that was terrorizing the village, but my mind refused to accept the validity of the question. My mind just couldn't accept that a spirit inhabited an animal. It was against all my learning. I was a man of logic.

"Yes, listen to your mind!" — a voice rang out loud in my head. "Nothing good will come if you are ruled by your heart. You are white. Your ways are different. Do not involve yourselves in the spirits of this land!"

Thus my mind agreed with her. The fog enveloped me again. I lost sight of the woman. Terror filled my being. I had the peculiar sensation of physical despair, of utter discomfort.

There was a noise. I felt the fog move and I was staring at the darkness of the verandah. The floorboards quivered again and I knew I was not alone. The old man had come to me.

"Did you meet her?" he asked me in a conspiratorial tone.

"No! It was just a dream," I insisted, relying on a barrage of rational thoughts and arguments.

The old man became impatient and accused me of being inflexible in my thinking. "You made the decision not to see! You have lost the capacity to feel, to see through your heart. Do you think your logic rules this world? Open your eyes. Don't hide behind your books like a child shielding itself behind its mother's skirt!"

The old man became increasingly furious. His wrinkled skin looked even more aged and he seemed to hunch. "Then, it's finished. You are no use to us. Leave in the morning. Follow the stream, it will take you to the village. Go back to your country, because we are people of the heart, not of the mind."

Dawn came much earlier than I expected. I searched for the old man to say goodbye, but he was nowhere to be found.

I followed the stream and, as he had said, it led me to the outskirts of the village. I walked into the village. The kampung folk looked at me in stony silence. I greeted a few of them, but they just stared at me as if I were a two-headed snake or some other monster. Anyway, I was quite fed up with their superstitions. They could believe what they wanted. It had nothing to do with me. But deep within me, the old man's words burned bitterly. "Then… You are no use to us." What had he meant?

My mind was plagued with a thousand questions, but there was nobody to answer them.

I found my tent burned to the ground, and my belongings scattered. Picking up my haversack, I slowly packed it with what I could lay hands on. The villagers stood at a distance, staring at me. Thank heavens, there would be a boat coming for me later in the day. I distinctly felt that I had outworn my welcome. How silly of them. I could have taught them many things, but if this was how they wanted it, this was the way it would be. It was their loss.

Holding my head high, I made my way to the river bank to wait. I considered all the events that had happened. I decided that the old man on the hill had tried to confuse me.

Over the jungle sounds, I heard the soft vibrations of the approaching boat. Its engine slowly grew louder, and the boat rounded the bend and came into full view. I climbed onto the jetty and slowly walked to the end. A boatman threw a rope and pulled the boat closer to the jetty. I didn't want to waste time, so even before he could tie the boat up, I had jumped onto the deck. The crewman took my haversack, while the Chinese captain beckoned me into the wheelhouse.

After exchanging greetings with me, he bent down and carefully brought out a half bottle of Johnnie Walker Red Label and poured generously into two tumblers, one of which he handed to me.

"Cheers," he toasted.

"Cheers," I replied; but there was no enthusiasm in my voice.

"So, what happened at the kampung, tuan?"

"Nothing much. It was not successful. The hill behind the village did not have many samples," I lied.

"You mean, you went up the hill. There got mad man."

"I met him. He speaks very good English."

"No! No!" the captain exclaimed. "He born deaf and dumb. Only know the ways of the spirits. Cannot talk. No hear, no talk!"

Born deaf and dumb. What utter nonsense!

It was then that the peculiar sensation of physical despair, of utter discomfort had begun. A feeling that has been with me ever since. A feeling that grows increasingly heavy, even as I sit in the garden of the Raffles Hotel.

'Stengah' in Raffles

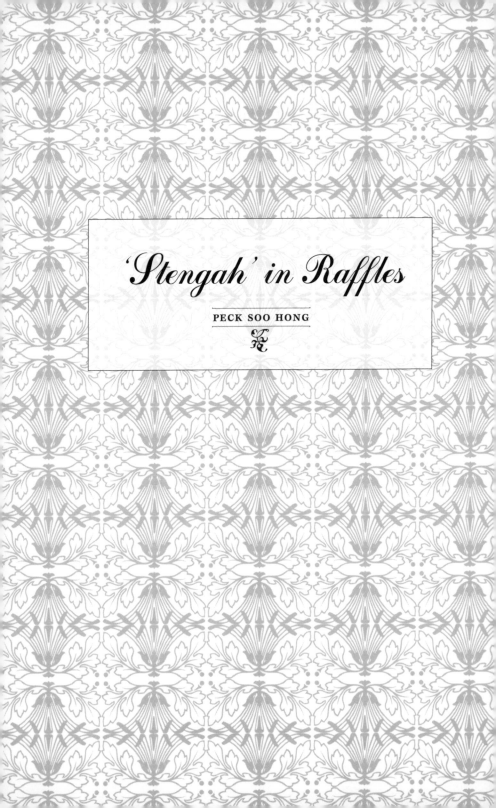

PECK SOO HONG

I AM Evelyn Misculy, born 84 years ago today, the sixth of June 1994. This is my happiest day because I am again seated in the famed Tiffin Room at the Raffles. From as long ago as 1923 I remember that famous quotation about the food, and how the Tiffin Room trumpeted Kipling's advice: "Feed at Raffles". I am truly at my happiest: spending my birthday, *and* witnessing my grand-daughter's engagement party going on, in the Raffles. No one has taken any notice of me. I am in the far end corner, inconspicuous, unobtrusive. Merely waiting for the entry of Evette and her fiancé.

As a child I had heard of Raffles. All of us knew that Raffles, like the Singapore Cricket Club and the Tanglin Club, was a haunt of the wealthy and the privileged. I have also heard of the visits by well-known writers, Somerset Maugham for one, who had actually stayed in Suite 77! In 1959 at the age of

85 he was on his way to Japan for the opening of an exhibition. He stayed in Suite 77 and would have been furiously writing away in a corner of the Palm Court. Oh, the excitement of stepping on the pavements once walked by him and other famous authors, Noel Coward and even Kipling! The very idea had been such a thrill to me then and is even now. Yes, I used to be known as an avid reader, besotted with tales of mysteries and intrigues.

When I grew up and was in my teens, being a Eurasian was nothing to be proud of at that time. Eurasians were contemptuously known as 'stengah', a word which means half — suggestive of a lower caste. In those days of old, 'stengah' also referred to a small whisky.

How I had longed to visit the Raffles. I hankered for the places where rituals of colonial life, like tea-dances and tiffin, were practised. But there was no way in which I could gain entry to the Raffles, meant exclusively for the white tuans. My mother had warned me to keep clear of the place. I remembered telling her that I was even willing to marry a white tuan so that I could visit the Raffles. She laughed; and then sadly told me that under no circumstances would I be allowed in. For any Englishman to marry me, he would be socially ostracised. Not only that. He would probably be sent back to where he had come from! Yes, and in disgrace too.

What could I do except read and dream about the silly white French-Renaissance-style building? I found out that 'she' was known as "the belle of Beach Road". The area around the Esplanade then, was designated a European Town, and Raffles was originally the first house on the famous row of twenty houses along Beach Road. It was opened as a hotel in 1886. There were stories told and passed on — and being a curious person, as I was, I was falling deeper in love with the building and was growing obsessive with wanting to know more. I had heard of her billiard rooms, which of course were as essential as the swimming pools of today. It seemed too cruel to deprive a girl, with such curiosity and a strong mind, of a visit. So I had to plan my own visitation. It was the timely encounter with John Done which sealed my fate. Yes, John Done! Strange name. It sounded like the famous metaphysical poet, John Donne. But Done was in no way related to the other Donne. If he had been perhaps then he would not have been 'undone'!

It was after the war. Sometime in 1946. I was in my mid-thirties. To be a woman, to be of that age and still unmarried, was considered scandalous. What could I do — for it was not the want of suitors? I had had my share of good-looking young men who would pursue me from church to church, from party to party; but it seemed as if fate would not have me wedded off to one of our local boys.

I must have been a snob. I considered them insipid, immature, iniquitous, injudicious. What I wanted was a man who was inimitable and independent and who had initiative. All the 'I's' in the man I was searching for were not to be found. So I had given up hope for marriage, much to the worry and chagrin of both my parents.

Relatives and friends too became concerned and embarrassed when they remembered I was still single. Gradually I hated attending parties and grew to enjoy my own company. I was not a bad looker, truly, for I had fair skin — taking after my mother. I also had a pair of beautiful, sparkling brown eyes and rather high-set cheek bones. I was also tallish and had long, naturally curved eyelashes. I was not ashamed of my looks for I believed I was endowed with attractive features. Perhaps it was because of my own high self-esteem that I had difficulty 'getting' a suitable husband. Whenever I met a match, I would challenge and ask questions by the dozen. Then I would request him to accompany me to the Raffles. No man then had ever dared take up the challenge, and so who could be surprised at me for remaining single at 36? Then it happened! I met him. My very own, darling Done.

I was dressed in my best Sunday clothes and was walking along the Esplanade. I was happy to, for I could pass as a European, if I was not scrutinised long enough. I strolled along the sea front. It was late evening. The dying sun cast its glow upon the shimmering water and I was enthralled by the beauty and the serenity. I then decided to sit down on one of the wrought iron benches. I had never done that before. It had always been a brisk walk through the Esplanade, merely taking in the balmy air. And, if courage took over, I would sometimes do a quick march down the Esplanade, right to the corner of Beach Road and steal glimpses of the Raffles. When no fierce 'jagas' lurked around, I would linger slightly longer, and try peering into the mysterious depths to spy on the inhabitants — and wild tales would spin around my giddy head.

On that particular evening, I was emboldened. The ambience of the place and the setting sun called out to me. Being a woman, I was intuitive. I had a strong urge to remain there. It was as if something was about to take place. I could not understand my own emotions nor my courage in staying longer than usual. Firstly, I was a Eurasian; and secondly, no decent woman would be on her own at that time of day! I was engrossed by the scene, enraptured by the cool breeze. I was in dreamland, almost.

"Hey you! What are you doing here?" A rough voice intruded into my peace.

I blinked and looked up. I saw a man in uniform. A policeman. As I failed to answer his question, he was turning aggressive. Must be that he saw that I was no white tuan's woman. He stared at me and asked if I had any form of identification. I was furious. Even at that time I was no gentle dame. I felt I had every right to be there. After all, Singapore belonged to me, as well!

My cheeks flushed and I felt anger choking my throat. Somehow, I was no longer terrified. But before I could say anything, I felt a presence. Then a deep resonant voice spoke out, "Is anything the matter, Officer? This lady is with me. We were enjoying the cool air."

The audacity! I was not his companion. But I certainly admired his suavity, his style, which reminded me of a Gary Cooper movie. I decided to go along with the make-believe. I gave the officer the sweetest of my smiles.

"Sorry, sir… I was merely doing my duty, sir… sorry…"

But he was interrupted: "It's OK. Anyone can make a mistake. Go along then. We will be getting along as well. We have a table reservation at the Raffles. Come, my dear." His almost-emerald eyes plunged into my soul and I knew that if I were to cast my eyes at his I would be lost. But I did not want LIFE to pass me by. When could I be given the chance again, to experience that sudden surge of hot emotions — so very strong that my usually stable legs were turning into soft putty? I took my chance and looked back into his pair of fathomless emerald whirlpools. And I fell in love! I knew then as I know now that that was the moment when my cynical heart was shot by Cupid's arrow. Despite the sudden warmth which had crept into my body, I felt a chill growing in my stomach. I was tongue-tied. I stared at him. He smiled and spoke in a most assuring manner, "You all right? You didn't mind my interfering, I hope? But he was pretty rude. I saw you sitting there, at peace and beautiful. And I hated him for questioning. It was too insulting."

How I wanted to impress him. To make the right utterances. But the voice that came out from me was a mouse-like squeak! "Thank you. I'll be going now. I should not be here."

"Why?" Then he came forward, almost imposing himself on me. He looked down at me and said in his persuasive tone, "We are going for dinner. You can't have me lying? I've told the officer we are having dinner."

What could I do? I had always felt tall and yet,

standing next to him, he was even taller. And here was the very challenge that I had been searching for all my life. He wanted to take me to the Raffles for dinner! What if they found out that I was not a European, though?

I floundered and stammered, "Perhaps, you had better not do so... I'm not..."

"A white woman?" he completed the statement. "I know. But you are an unusual local. Brave, and independent too. I like that. We will fool everyone. We will have the most sumptuous dinner!" And he was insistent. Not that I could refuse either. I had always wanted to go into the place, and the opportunity was opened at long last: after waiting for nearly 30 years.

Yes, we had the most wonderful, glorious dinner. The soft music wafting into the room, the ladies each so elegantly dressed, the men so gentle and polite. The ambience of the place, the magic of the night and the hero next to me transported me as if into a castle, and I was a princess — lost in a dream world.

How clearly I remember the events and the emotional strands which pulled at my soul on that night. It has been said that you are really elderly when you can remember only the past with vividness, and cannot recall the most recent incident. Oh, yes, I remember every detail of that night, across almost fifty years. He introduced himself as John Done. He took me onto the dance floor after dinner, and later drove me home in his car. He was a pilot in the Royal Air Force, stationed in Singapore for a few years.

Before that night was over, he had completely won me. To hear him say that I had overwhelmed him sounded so bizarre. Yet he repeatedly said, "You are so enchanting. I have never met anyone, seen anyone, like you. Especially when I recall you sitting down on the Esplanade — and then becoming adventurous. If I were a painter I would capture your very soul on canvas. It was perfect. The woman, the glorious sunset, the moving, fluffy clouds and the lapping sounds of the sea." He sighed with satisfaction. How weird, I thought. It must have been the stengah he was drinking!

But he was so genuine, so intrigued by what I said that I was beginning to believe whatever he told me.

That was the start of our friendship, and within weeks it turned into the most talked about romance in Katong. I was then living in Marshall Road. And when he came with his 'armoured car' (as the people in Marshall Road termed it), eyes would pop and tongues would wag. My dear parents warned me of the eventual heartbreak, for they knew that one day he would have to return. But I was young and in love. I thought Done's love for me would stand against all odds and that eventually he would make me Mrs Done. Foolish heart of mine! But I have no regret. I never became Mrs Done, but I had a lovely daughter. A daughter conceived out of our intense love *and* out of wedlock! Such a scandal at that time! Done could not marry me. Being in love we grew careless in our daily contact. We appeared at functions where he was invited — for the mere idea of an evening's separation, even for a few hours, was unbearable. Love really enslaved us and we lapped up every moment we shared together. It could be because our love was forbidden that we wanted society to accept it. But the society he was brought up in was not ready to accept a stengah into their world of class, appearances, snobbery: upper crust and stiff upper-lipped! Poor Done could not survive the onslaught of criticism, sneers, whispers and innuendoes. We both knew that sooner or later he would receive his re-posting order. The authorities definitely wanted to keep their officers away from the 'locals'. To safeguard and uphold the 'good' name of the RAF, he was posted back to England and 'home'.

I can no longer remember clearly the events after that. It is said that one's mind only wants to store up good things. Sad times would be automatically shut out! Yet I know there was the missing of a 'body' — a person, whom you love more than life itself, being plucked away. I did not know how I managed to survive. All the gossip, the hatred, the misunderstanding I had to endure. Friends turned into foes, and suddenly I was all alone to face my own problems. I was with his child — and I never regretted having Annette.

She grew into a beautiful woman, and eventually she looked after me. She knew she was a bastard; but like me was able to stand up to society's criticism. Born of love, she was headstrong and determined to prove that people were wrong to pass judgment, and that each one must follow his own destiny. She was not a conformist; and she was a survivor, like me. She never got to meet her father though. A real pity. For they would simply have loved each other.

Time passed. With the passing of time, memory fades further. But I recall one incident most vividly. I was 52 years old then. Life in Singapore had changed tremendously. We had our independence, we sang our own National Anthem instead of God Save The King or Queen, we were building our own Singaporean identity. We were four races living in harmony. There were no stengahs and anyone with cash could go anywhere. But Raffles had somewhat lost her past glory and splendour. I was so very happy that, in 1972, the Preservation of Monuments Board was started — and showed concern in identifying, inspecting and overseeing buildings which had contributed to the architectural heritage of Singapore. Raffles was saved from a lingering death. She was gradually reconstructed, refurbished, restored and brought back to her splendid old charm.

I cannot remember much more. But here I am sitting so comfortably. The hotel is definitely more comfortable now than before.

Strange that I should be thinking of the past. But then what do the dead ponder on? After all, when we die what future is there?

Yes, I have long been dead. I was given the opportunity to make a wish because it is my birthday. And I requested to re-visit Raffles, to 're-live' the high point of my past. Besides I wanted to see my granddaughter, whom I did not meet in life. I am glad to have made the request for, as I speak in my mind, I can see John. And he is not old but the same young, handsome, dashing hero who once swept me off my feet. The one with whom I knew what love was and how powerful it could be!

Ah, here comes the bridal party. There she is. So pure, so sweet and so like her mother, Annette, my darling girl. I can see you both so clearly. Touch you and call your names. But you cannot come into my world, the world of the dead.

I shall go away happy. What a birthday it has been. I

will wait for next year; and, who knows, I could be allowed another special request! Where we are now, we only live for that one day a year! Goodbye, darlings.

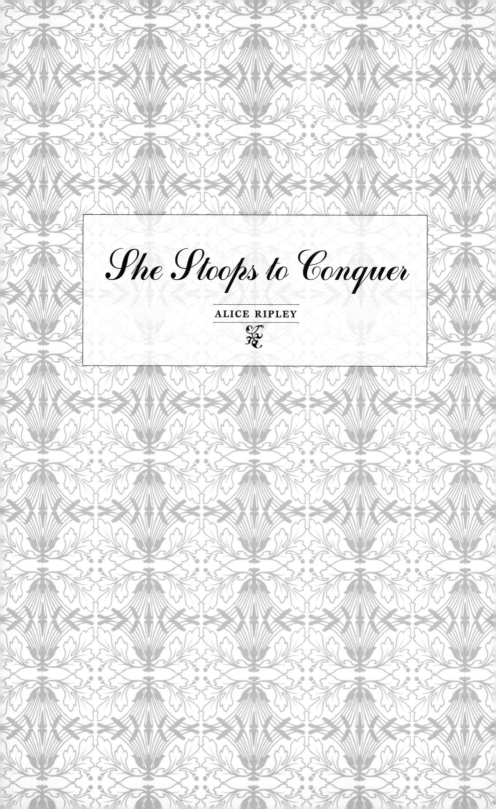

She Stoops to Conquer

ALICE RIPLEY

SHE was upper-class, there was no doubt. She attracted the most discerning of men and women.

Her limousine pulled into the Beach Road entrance of Raffles Hotel. The doorman in his elegant uniform smiled. She was as pretty as the orchids cascading out of their pots. She had enjoyed a good education, studying at Stanford not far from the family's vineyard in Napa Valley, California. She was young, probably twenty-six, recently married to Y. S. Wong, who spent most of his time in China, marketing telecommunications. She was lucky to be in Singapore with him this trip as the last six months were spent alone in Hong Kong while he worked on his already vast empire. Her name was Moe.

Their luggage with the distinctive green and maroon stripes was taken most carefully, and they entered the marvellous lobby. Moe had studied art and architecture, and conscientiously swept her trained eyes over the impeccable restoration: the grand staircase, the windows and wood polished with pride. The bellhops standing at attention did not miss her assessment, which pleased them very much.

Y. S. and Moe were ushered to their suite. It was done up in white and yellow, matching the Singapore sun which poured in through the sparkling windows. The huge bed was covered in a yellow and white orchid print with ten or twelve pillows plumped, making it very inviting. Charming Louis XV chairs flanked a fireplace, holding greenery instead of wood. The creamy white leather sofas were off to the left. All in all, it was very splendid.

"Darling, I hope to spend time with you this evening. Will you be all right until six o'clock tonight?" asked Y. S.

"Of course, Y. S. There are shops here to let me spend some of that money you keep pulling in," Moe said, laughing as she unpacked her gowns and robes. "I must find the best restaurant today and we will spend the evening billing and cooing. I know I'll be happy as a dove, at Raffles," she said.

She went into the bathroom and looked at herself in the mirror. What she saw was not only her bronzed, shiny skin, but her black-as-the-night-sky perfectly-trimmed hair in a China-doll cut. In the mirror the black and white marble reflected the gold plated fixtures. Sunshine-yellow towels, thick and puffy, overflowed from the gold racks. The sunken tub had jets and faucets poking out of the massive enclosure. She removed her horizontal black-and-white-striped knit dress, and pulled on her white silk shirt and pants. She took a small, elegant straw hat with a red chequered sash around the crown. She slipped into leather thongs and started out to shop, after saying goodbye to Y. S.

Moe went to the shops around the outer edge on the Bras Basah Road side first. She noticed a handsome elderly gentleman dressed in a black and white batik shirt. He had a small jar which looked as if it contained paste wax. He was giving the final touches of polish to the white painted window sill, using a tooth brush.

Moe peeped through the various windows and went into the gift shop. She found it delightful, and after much studying of the wares she bought a jar of papaya-and-coconut jam to tuck away, maybe for a gift. She bought antique reproductions of luggage labels and perused the beautiful book on the history of Raffles.

She chose a small pewter piece for her father's desk from the Royal Selangor shop. The saleslady wrapped it for her in midnight-blue paper. There were some lovely people shopping in there from Italy. Moe conversed in her excellent Italian about skiing in the Italian Alps and the wonderful taste of Northern Italian cuisine. She said "ciao", and took the escalator to the second floor.

Moe was charmed by the Blue Ginger shop, and bought several outfits for her two younger sisters. She was so impressed because the batik fabric was created in Singapore.

Moe was rather restless after her tour of the shops. She started back to her room taking a back lift. As she walked down the hall on the third floor she noticed a large Philippine-mahogany louvred door. She tried the elegant brass door knob and it opened. Inside, it was cool and dark except for a small outside window that had the sun casting its bright rays across the fairly large shelves holding golden towels and dozens of white percale sheets, neatly folded.

"Hmm, what a sight, just a storage unit." She paused for thought. After a little more looking around, she noticed — on a brass hook, just behind the wooden shelves — a uniform. It was a yellow and white striped dress, with a lacy apron tied around the top of the hanger. On the side of the dress at the waist was a safety pin holding a key.

"Oh, my, I wonder if this is a master key," she

mused. "How careless of someone."

She decided to try the garment on. "Just for fun: I'll see what it feels like to be in a uniform," she thought.

It was just a lark, really. She, of course, had many maids and a butler in Hong Kong. She slipped off her white shirt and trousers, and slipped into the dress. She noticed a faint, sweet smell of the owner's — maybe sandalwood — incense. It did seem strange to feel the soft, ironed cotton touching her skin, as she always, wore silk next to her body. She had no way of seeing what she looked like. She decided to take a short walk to her suite so that she could look in a mirror. She might even take a picture of herself in the glass, just for the fun of it. She walked out of the door, tying the apron, and started for her room. Before you could even say "Cartier", someone yelled at her.

"Hey, you lazy lah. Take this tray to the Empress kitchen. It's been sitting here forever. Take it now lah."

Moe was astonished. They were talking to her as a maid.

"Good God, how do I get out of this?" thought Moe. "I'll just take the tray over there and then sneak back to the closet, change clothes and get my packages."

She walked to the kitchen. The aroma of onions, garlic and oil wafted up. The chefs, with big white hats and white clogs, were busy stirring huge pots of steamy dishes. A little further down were the dishwashers. A couple of waiters were adjusting their black ties, the tuxedo jackets draped over chairs.

"Ah, good-looking, you're new. Where have you been?" one of the waiters shouted.

Moe shuddered. "This is awful. How do I get out of this?" her brain asked again.

At that moment a young apprentice came through a swinging door with another tray, colliding with her. Their trays, dishes and silver jingled to the floor, landing with a crash.

"Kacee lah. You pin twah!"† someone shouted.

"Who are you lah? You are new but you have a pass key. You must know better than to stand at that door," shouted someone else.

Moe, almost in tears from embarrassment, told them the truth. How she found the uniform, how she was just going to take a peek at herself — and was ordered to take the tray to the kitchen.

A senior chef looked up and eyed her sternly. He walked over, wooden spoon held high. "You are a guest? What is your favourite food?" he asked. Silence. "What?" he bellowed.

"Oh, gosh, I love to eat laksa and prata." She said.

† "Kacee lah. You pin twah!" — "How dare you! Lazy person!"

She knew she should have left without answering; but she felt that would be offensive.

"Good," said the chef, "get yourself back where you belong and we will serve it to you this evening."

The waiters were laughing.

Moe was escorted to her room by one of the butlers. He returned with her packages, and took the yellow and white shell of a dress. He told her the maid who left it unlocked would be spoken to but would be retained. He hesitated for a moment and said kindly to Moe, "Somerset Maugham wrote, a long time ago, that Raffles stands for all the fables of the exotic East. I think your experience today comes into that category. You had a taste of hard work, and I hope you have learned from it." When she had locked the room door behind him, she fell onto her bed and wept.

That evening, Moe showered, powdered and primped. Y. S. looked wonderful in his summer linen, and took her to the Empress Room. Moe dazzled in a black sheath. In her hand she held a red friendship flower.

The waiters, smart and crisp, smiled — no, beamed when she arrived. A chorus of greetings came across the room.

"Hello, Moe."

"Hi, Miss Moe."

"Welcome, Moe."

They were seated, surrounded by waiters flapping napkins in the air for their laps.

The maitre d' said, "Madam Moe, dinner is served."

Y. S. looked puzzled and asked how she knew all these people and how they knew what both of them wanted to eat.

Moe laughed and said, "Let's just say I bumped into them today."

Do you have a story to tell about Raffles?

WE WOULD have achieved what we set out to do if these tales inspire others to relate their encounters with the Grand Old Lady of Singapore. If we receive an interesting enough collection, we will publish a follow-up to this book. You may like to call us for more information before you send your stories to:

Fables from the Raffles Hotel Arcade
Raffles Hotel Arcade
328 North Bridge Road
Singapore 0718
Tel: 65-3371886

Please do not forget to include your name and address.

The stories, which must be original and unpublished, should not be longer than 3,000 words although it can be much shorter if you think that works best.

THE PUBLISHER